BEAUTY IN FLIGHT

BEAUTY IN FLIGHT BOOK 1

ROBIN PATCHEN

JDO PUBLISHING

For my sister, Jennifer.
My playmate, my secret-keeper, my champion.
No matter how far apart we live, you'll always be my best friend.

CHAPTER ONE

Two years out should have been enough. Cell mates no longer shoved her, fellow inmates no longer raised their fists, and guards no longer leered. A year ago, she'd been released from parole. Harper Cloud was free.

Except her heart didn't believe it.

At least the icky, creepy, somebody's-watching-me sensation she'd had since she'd left her house that afternoon faded as soon as she walked through the doors of the nursing home. Among these beautiful residents, Harper felt safer than she did anywhere else in the world.

"Harper, Miss Estelle's asking for you." Teresa, the LPN who worked the six-to-two shift, tossed the words over her shoulder as she lumbered behind the counter at the nurses' station.

"She feeling all right?"

"As good as can be, all things considered." Teresa typed something into the computer, then looked at Harper again. "New guy in Room 104. Peanut allergy."

"Got it." Harper had been trained as an LPN and had once hoped to become a registered nurse. Prison had changed all that. She was lucky to have landed this job as a nursing assistant. While she delivered meals, mopped floors, cleaned bedpans, she focused on how much she loved caring for the elderly, these patients who'd become her closest friends, and ignored the fact that she barely made enough to pay her bills. She helped Mr. Jenkins to the restroom and pushed away a moment of self-pity. She was free to work where she chose. So what if she had to work weekends at the grocery store to pay for the classes she was taking at the local community college? Money wasn't important to her. Being free—that was what mattered. And the feeling of safety was certainly a plus.

But was it an illusion?

The fear she'd walked to work with tried to worm its way into her mind, but she pushed it away. In here, among her friends, she was safe.

After she checked on all the other patients, she pushed into Miss Estelle's room. "How you feeling today?"

The old woman's wrinkled face split into a big smile, and Harper raised the bed so Estelle could sit up. Her puffy blue-gray hair was flattened on one side from a recent catnap. Her brown eyes sparkled in her pale skin. "I wondered when you'd finally get around to me."

Harper leaned in and kissed the woman's cheek. Estelle looked grayer today. The pneumonia had taken a lot out of her. "You're not my only patient, Estelle, just my favorite. You need anything?"

"Went to the bathroom all by myself just a few minutes ago." Harper tried to show her disapproval with a glare, but Estelle only laughed and waved toward the chair beside her bed. "Been doing it since before you were a twinkle in your daddy's eyes. Sit down, honey."

Harper glanced at the door, then took the chair. "Just for a minute."

"But you saved me for last, right?"

"Don't I always? Everybody's settled. Now, tell me. What'd the doctor say?"

"Pfft." She waved off the question as if it were a black fly. "Told me I'm on the mend, but we know better than that."

Estelle's hand was cold when Harper took it. "Don't say that. If he says you're improving—"

"We both know I'm not long for this world. I'm not complaining. I'm ready to go home."

The thought of this place, of the world, without Estelle made Harper's eyes prickle. She was the closest thing to family Harper had. "This is your home." Her voice cracked on the last word, and she looked down, blinking furiously.

Estelle squeezed Harper's hand. "You listen to me, honey."

Harper looked up and sniffed.

"I love you, too. You're a good girl."

Harper started to protest, but the woman's grip tightened, silencing her. "Don't you argue with me. I'm an old woman, and I know what I'm talking about. You're not perfect. You've made mistakes. Join the club. But you got a God who loves you and wants you back. And you got a family who loves you—"

"They don't."

Estelle stared at her with those aged brown eyes. "They're not perfect, either. So they screwed up. You never going to forgive them, after everything?"

"I don't have to forgive them, Estelle. I'm the one who went to prison."

"And they should have been there for you. That's what family does. They screwed it up, and I bet they know it now. Call your mother, hon. I promise she wants to hear from you."

Hot tears dripped onto their gripped hands. "As soon as I have something to tell her. As soon as I... as I feel like I'm worthy—"

"Worthy. Pfft. You think you can do something to make yourself worthy? What did you do to make your folks love you when you were born? You earn that somehow?"

The question threw her off. "When I was an infant? What could I do?"

"Nothing. You were probably cute, but mothers even love their ugly babies. Babies do nothing to earn love. They scream and poop and eat." Estelle chuckled. "Not that I do much more than that now."

"Stop that. You're—"

"The point is, nobody's worthy. Or maybe everybody is. I don't know. I only know your mom doesn't need you to be perfect. She just wants you home."

Harper pictured her mother, the disappointment on her face that last time Harper had seen her. Mom and Dad had come to Vegas to surprise her and had gone to the club where she'd been a dancer. That's how she'd described her job to them, but they'd figured out what she really did by looking at the posters of the nearly naked women on the blacked-out windows. Her parents hadn't gone inside, thank God. But they knew what she'd become. The shame, the horror had been written all over their faces. And that was before Harper'd gone to prison.

"You have to give them another chance," Estelle said.

The desire to hear her mother's voice was so strong that she considered calling right then. But their last conversation ricocheted in her brain like a gunshot. She'd called from the jail right after they'd taken her into custody. Her father's words had never been far from her mind. "Don't call here again. Ever."

So she hadn't. What was there to say? *Hey guys, I'm not a stripper anymore. Drugs...? Kicked that habit. Prison was a long time ago. I know I said I was going to become a nurse, but I love my minimum wage job.* No, she wouldn't call them, not until she had something worthwhile to report. She wouldn't call until she could tell them something they could be proud of. Assuming she ever called at all.

The fact that she had a huge hole in her heart seemed irrelevant but fair, all things considered.

Estelle let go of her hand and coughed again and again. She couldn't seem to stop.

Harper helped her lean forward, soothing her until she could breathe again. Finally, Estelle lay back and took a few breaths.

"Should I get the nurse?"

Estelle shook her head, recovering a moment longer. Harper busied herself tidying the room. When she'd tossed the last of the tissues that hadn't quite made it into the trash, she said, "I'll go and let you rest."

"One more thing." Estelle paused to take another deep breath.

Harper returned to her spot at the beside, and Estelle turned her piercing eyes on Harper once again. "On your way here, did you get the feeling again?"

The fear came back like a bad virus. "I shouldn't have told you about that."

"Honey, God gave you instincts for a reason. You trust 'em. You think somebody's following you, then you take care, protect yourself. You get that pepper spray like I told ya?"

"I keep it in my pocket when I'm walking alone."

"Good, good." The woman reached toward the end table on the far side of her bed and snatched a cardboard box barely big enough to hold a lighter. "I got you this."

Harper took the box. "How did you—?"

"Amazon. They got everything. Open it."

Harper broke the seal at the end of the box and slid out the contents. She slid the keyring over her finger. Dangling from it was a Swiss Army knife about two inches long.

"Go ahead," Estelle said.

Harper pried out the small blade and showed Estelle. What was she supposed to do with this?

"It won't kill anybody, but it'll hurt like the dickens if you stab somebody with it."

"I could never—"

"Yeah, you're too sweet for your own good. But you do as I say. The mace in one pocket, the knife in the other. And don't be scared to use either one if you need to. Got it?"

"Yes, ma'am."

"Don't *ma'am* me. I'm not that old." The woman started to laugh, but it turned into a cough.

Harper stood. "Let me get someone."

But Estelle grabbed her hand and shook her head. When she'd settled again, Harper said, "Where I come from, we *ma'am-and-sir* our elders."

"Kansas." Estelle clucked her tongue as if being from Kansas were akin to being from Jupiter. "Just can't imagine. Now, tell me about your young man. Have you made a decision?"

Harper sighed. "I don't want to leave you."

"Nonsense." Estelle's New York accent came out more when she was vehement. "The question is, do you love him?"

"I don't know." Harper pictured Derrick Burns, his kind eyes, his gentle demeanor. "He's nice to me. We have great conversations on the phone. When we're together, it's as if I'm the only person in his whole world."

"You feel that way about him?"

She'd been burned by so many guys, it was hard to trust. "Maybe, someday."

"Hmph." Estelle pinned Harper with her gaze. "But you'd leave your stalker here. Surely he wouldn't follow you across the country."

"I don't have a stalker."

"Don't you poo-poo it. Even if not for the creep following you, there's the job. If it doesn't work out with the guy, the job would be good. You gotta think of your future."

"Assuming Derrick wouldn't fire me if we broke up."

"That'd be up to his grandfather, though. Not your boyfriend. And you'll win over the old man in about five minutes. Then, whatever happens with Derrick, at least you'll have that job."

"Is it wrong to go there for the job, not for him?"

"It's not like he proposed. Right?"

"He just wants me closer to him so he doesn't have to come to Vegas to see me."

"What's wrong with Vegas? It's a far sight better than where he's from. Who wants all that cold and rain and humidity, anyway?"

Harper didn't argue with Estelle, but after living in Las Vegas for years, she'd tired of the heat and sunshine. There were days she longed for cloudy and rainy and cold. Those kinds of days made the sunny ones that much more special. No, it wasn't moving to Maryland that made Harper hesitate. And to work as a private nurse for a wealthy old man would be much better than this job, even if she did love her patients. The job would be the first step in claiming the life she wanted—a real job, one her parents could be proud of.

If she moved to Maryland, she'd live with Derrick's grandfather rent-free and have the money to attend college and finish her Bachelor's degree. Assuming she could ever figure out what she wanted to do with her life now that being an RN was off the table. She wasn't going back to performing. She knew too well where that path led.

But what about Derrick? He'd sworn he didn't have expectations for their relationship, but she'd never met a man who didn't give without expecting something in return. What would he expect from her?

Right now, he acted as if she were his lifeline. He called her every night before bed and again on his way to work every morning. Flew to Vegas to visit her every chance he got.

"You're my anchor," he'd told her. "My salvation."

The words worried her. She could barely take care of herself. How could she be another person's salvation?

And what did he need to be saved from?

But every reservation was drowned under the sea of gifts and flowers and words of devotion.

She took Estelle's hand. It was wrinkled and cold. "I can't imagine leaving you."

"I got a date with Jesus, and I think it's coming soon."

"Don't say that."

When the old woman laughed, her face glowed, and Harper

saw the young beauty she'd surely been. "I'm not afraid to die, Harper. Dying's the easy part. It's living that's hard. You gotta figure out how to live." Estelle squeezed Harper's fingers. "Not for a guy, not to feed and wipe the bottoms of a bunch of old people. You need to figure out how to live for you."

CHAPTER TWO

I was after ten that night when Harper bid Estelle and the rest of her patients good-night and left the nursing home. She hated walking alone after dark, hated the fear that haunted her. She'd been saving for a car and could almost afford a decent junker. But not yet.

She hitched her purse onto her shoulder and stuck one hand in her jacket pocket to grip the pepper spray. The other hand closed over her new key chain. Wouldn't Estelle be proud?

Air that had been hot earlier had dropped to the fifties. There were people about, despite the late hour and the fact that it was a Wednesday. Nightlife never ended in Las Vegas. She was thankful for all the city lights and thankful that the Las Vegas nightlife had played a part in her meeting Derrick.

A few months before, exhausted from a long night of partying with his friends, he'd come to the grocery store where she worked weekends. He'd chatted with her and taken her to breakfast. Something had clicked. They'd talked for hours that day. It had been the start of a conversation that never seemed to end. She'd told him the truth about her past, and he'd hardly blinked. It had made her nervous, the way he'd accepted her so quickly, but over the months she'd known him, those nerves had been buried beneath his acts of kindness.

Sometimes, she wanted to slow things down with Derrick. Other times, she wanted desperately to escape this life she was leading, and Derrick seemed like the answer. He'd been begging her for months to move to Maryland to take care of his grandfather. It was too soon, though. Wasn't it? To move across the country for a guy she barely knew?

A guy, she thought... Could she love him? Could she ever trust a man again after her last boyfriend? Emmitt had ruined her life.

It was probably the thought of her ex-boyfriend that had the hair on her arms standing on end. A feeling that someone was there, someone was watching, waiting. The fear that had plagued her for months, years, prickled her skin.

Foolishness, of course. She hadn't reconnected with any of her friends from before—not that they'd been real friends, anyway. Back then, only Emmitt, her ex-boyfriend, and Barry, his best friend, had felt like true friends. Felt like it, but look what they'd gotten her into. Both of them were still in prison.

Aside from Derrick, Harper hadn't connected with anyone except Estelle since she'd been released. Oh, there were familiar faces on campus where she was taking a few classes, but those bright-eyed college students wouldn't want to be her friend if they knew the real Harper Cloud. They didn't have a past like hers. They didn't have her sins, her criminal record. Compared to her, they were innocent.

There was nobody in Vegas who cared enough about Harper to follow her. She'd been telling herself that for weeks. She was safe. Of course she was safe.

Adrenaline flooded her veins anyway.

She walked faster, past a loud group of tourists who smelled of cigarettes and marijuana and liquor. Since prison, she had no desire for that kind of life. She passed an off-the-strip hotel, where the dings and beeps of the slot machines in the lobby carried through the open door, she kept her head down and crossed the street.

The fear crossed with her.

The sound of footsteps behind her seemed to get louder, closer, until they pounded in her ears.

The narrow alley that led to the back door of her apartment building was just ahead. She could walk around to the front, but to get there she had to pass a very dark stretch of sidewalk before reaching the floodlights and street traffic. Or she could cut through the alley.

A stalker could hurt her on the sidewalk or in the alley.

She'd be inside faster if she cut through the alley.

She was crazy. Nobody was following her. This insanity had to stop. Whoever was behind her was just a tourist or one of the millions of workers who kept this town running. This feeling was just her own anxiety chasing her like demons, mocking her. She was fine. She was safe. She was practically invisible these days.

Outside the nursing home, nobody even saw her anymore.

Great. Now she was being maudlin.

She squared her shoulders and turned down the alley.

The footsteps followed.

Adjusting her key so it would be ready for the lock, she moved faster. She was nearly there when something moved at the far end of the alley. A man in the shadows walked toward her.

Two men were closing in. One behind, one in front.

Her hands were trembling by the time she reached the door. She tried to slide the key into the lock. Fumbled it, and the keys clattered to the concrete. She passed the pepper spray from her left hand to her right and started to turn. A hand clamped on her upper arm, kept the pepper spray aimed at his knees.

She gasped, desperate to scream but unable to force the sound past her terror.

"Hey!" A deep voice. A familiar voice. It came from the man on the far end of the alley. He was running their direction.

The man with his hand on her arm turned and bolted.

The other man, the one with the familiar voice, chased him.

Stunned, confused, she watched as the first man rounded the corner and disappeared. The second followed him.

She stared into the darkness.

Had that just happened?

Had she lost her mind, conjured danger where none existed?

Danger... and salvation?

She snatched her key from the asphalt, pepper spray still gripped in her fist.

Her hands trembled, slick with sweat, but she managed to slip her key into the lock on the outer door of her building. She was turning the knob when she heard footsteps again.

Please, no.

"Harper?"

She turned toward the familiar voice she'd heard before.

"Barry?"

He jogged down the alley and stopped beside her. "I thought that was you. I saw you walking..."

His words faded. Or maybe she did. Suddenly, the dark night got darker, and her legs turned to jelly. She gasped as if she hadn't taken a breath in minutes. Maybe she hadn't.

"Hey." Barry gripped her upper arms. "You okay? You look like you're about to pass out."

"If you hadn't been there..." But she couldn't finish the statement.

"But I was." He pulled her close and wrapped his arms around her back. "You're safe."

Safe. She was safe. She took a deep breath, straightened. She was all right. She'd survived worse.

He let her go, turned the knob, and pushed the door open. "This is your building?"

"I'm fine. I'll be okay now."

"I'm walking you to your door anyway. Just to be sure. What if that guy went around to the front and got someone to let him in?"

The thought had her heart dropping. "Okay. Thank you."

She led the way into the building and up the narrow staircase, down the hall and to the door of her tiny studio apartment. "Oh." She'd left her key dangling from the keyhole downstairs. When she turned to Barry, he lifted his hand, and her keyring hung from his index finger, her key swinging beside the new knife.

"Here"—he nodded to the keyhole—"let me."

She stepped out of the way while he unlocked her door and pushed it open.

"Thank you."

"I'm just glad I happened by when I did."

The hair on her arms rose. Nobody *happened by* this part of town. Just a few blocks off the strip, but it might as well have been miles and miles. Suspicion had her stepping into her apartment, never taking her eyes off him. She kept one hand on the doorknob, prepared to slam it shut. "What were you doing in the alley?"

His smile seemed natural enough. "I saw you at end of the block. I was on the other corner. I was going to cut through the alley, see if I could catch up with you. When you turned in, I wasn't sure if it was you or not. I was getting closer to make sure. Then I saw that guy behind you."

Seemed reasonable, but... "What were you doing on the street?"

"There's a little bar on the next block. I met some friends there. My car was parked in that lot on the corner."

The story sounded plausible. And it definitely hadn't been Barry following her into the alley. If Barry hadn't been there, she hated to think what would have happened.

She held out her hand, palm up, and he dropped the keys in it. "Will you be okay?"

She nodded, then shook her head. "I'm a little..." But she couldn't find the word.

"Discombobulated?"

The sudden chuckle surprised her. "Yeah. That."

"Want me to come inside, make sure it's safe?"

"No, no. I'm sure it's..." She cocked her head, focused on him again. "When did you get released?"

He shrugged. "They let me go. A technicality."

Let him go? He'd been convicted of accessory to murder. How could that have happened? "And Emmitt? Is he...?"

"He's still in."

Thank God. The last thing she needed was Emmitt back in her life. Or Barry, for that matter.

"How long have you been out?" she asked.

"Couple months. I got a good job developing apps for this..." He chuckled and ducked his head. "It doesn't matter. Suffice it to say, that part of my life is over." He took in her apartment, the little dinette set beside the tiny kitchen, the loveseat that faced the TV she'd bought used for fifty bucks, the twin bed, unmade, pushed against the far wall. "And what about you?"

"I work, I go to school, I work some more."

"Nursing?"

"You remember."

"You're hard to forget, Harper."

She ignored the remark, not sure what to make of it. "I'm taking general ed classes until I figure out what I want to do."

"You don't want to be an RN?"

"With a felony? I'm lucky I got hired as a nurse's assistant." She smiled, yawned. "I'm sorry. It's been a long day. I owe you so much more than a thank-you, but that's all I have to offer."

He took her hand in both of his. They were warm and clammy. "Please be careful. You can't be walking down alleys by yourself at night. It's not safe."

The memory of that man... How long had he been following her? What would he have done if Barry hadn't been there? "I know. You're right. Next time, I'll stick to the main roads and go in the front."

He tilted his head to the side. "No car?"

"I'm saving for one."

"You need—"

"I appreciate your concern, Barry. Truly. I'll manage." She showed him her pepper spray. "See, I had it well in hand."

He didn't even crack a smile. "If you ever need anything..." He reached in his pocket and pulled out a business card. It was crisp, professional. So was he. The long hair he'd worn before had been cut to a respectable length. He wore crisp trousers and a long-sleeved golf shirt, tucked in. He looked like the young professional he'd been before he fell in with Emmitt. Nobody would ever guess Barry was an ex-con.

Good looks were about as trustworthy as a heroin junkie.

She pictured Derrick, his smile. No. He was a good guy with a good job. He treated her like gold.

She took Barry's business card, though she knew she'd never call. He'd saved her tonight, no doubt. But Barry was in her past, and she didn't want to bring anything from that life into this one.

CHAPTER THREE

Harper was slipping on the oversize T-shirt she slept in when her phone rang. She snatched it up and crawled into bed. "Hey."

"You're home safe?" Derrick's voice brought tears she hadn't expected.

"I'm home."

A beat passed, then, "Did something happen?"

Was she really that easy to read over the phone and across the miles? "Sort of. When I was walking home..." She told him the story. Though he was silent on the other end, tension radiated through the phone. She finished with, "I'm safe now."

A moment passed. She held her breath, waited for his reaction.

Finally, he said, "That's it. I can't..." A deep breath. "I can't do this anymore. Harper, I care for you. I feel like you and me... We've both messed up, and we're not perfect, but I care about you more than you know. I need you. I feel like, with you on my side, I can do anything, conquer anything. You're my...my lifeline. My salvation." His words were pleading. "I'm terrified something is going to happen to you. And tonight—"

"I was fine. Tonight was an aberration." But even as she said the words, fear tingled up the back of her neck. Was Derrick the answer?

When he spoke again, his words were measured. Angry. "Tonight proves it. You're not safe there. It's time for you to come to Maryland."

The tone of his words, the vehemence behind them. Was she imagining the anger?

Of course she was. Derrick only wanted what was best for her. And as if to prove it, he blew out a long breath. "I'm sorry. I don't have any right to tell you what to do. But Gramps needs somebody to take care of him." Derrick's voice was back to its kind and considerate tone. "I don't think he's been taking his meds consistently. And I can't put off hiring a nurse any longer. I trust you. I want you taking care of him."

Derrick had told her all about his grandfather, certain she'd love him. But what about Derrick, could she love him? "I'm just not—"

"Not for me. Don't move here for me." Though she couldn't see him, she could imagine him pacing, running his fingers over his short hair. "I promise, I won't ask anything of you. I don't expect anything of you. Just... I need to know you're safe. Move here for you. To be safe. To keep my grandfather safe. To start fresh."

To start fresh. The words reverberated like a promise.

Estelle was right. Derrick was right. She'd never be able to start over if she stayed in this city filled with memories. She needed a fresh start. Derrick's job offer was the perfect solution.

"Harper...?"

"Yes."

"Yes, as in—?"

"As soon as I finish my exams and give my notice, I'll move to Maryland."

CHAPTER FOUR

Harper couldn't believe she'd actually done it. She'd sold most of her belongings and collected her security deposit. Then, she'd driven all the way across the country in a beat-up VW Jetta, praying as the car coughed and sputtered into a gas station in southern Utah, as the fan belt broke in Kansas, and when she needed a tire change during rush hour outside of Indianapolis, Indiana.

But she'd made it. And here she was.

Yes, she still missed Estelle. The woman had been right. A week after Harper told her she was moving, Estelle died in her sleep. Her last words, spoken earlier that very evening, had resonated with Harper ever since. "You've got a family who loves you, hon. But no matter what they say or do, you've got a God who loves you more, and always has."

She'd purchased a Bible the next day, and she'd been reading it ever since. It had become a good way to kill the long hours alone in motel rooms on her cross-country trek. She'd even bought a journal, which was mostly filled with questions about what she was reading.

Now here she was, driving a Cadillac, pulling up to the house that had become her home. The house was enormous, bigger than the four-bedroom she'd grown up in back in Kansas. The neighboring houses—all equally grand and pretty—weren't so close the neighbors could spy for evening entertainment. And the trees! After the barren sand of Las Vegas, the vegetation felt as lush as a jungle.

She marveled at her good fortune. How had she landed here, in this amazing place? Nobody deserved it less.

Maybe God really did love her.

"What's the holdup, girl?"

She turned to her passenger and smiled. "Just admiring the view."

Red Burns mashed the button to open the garage door, and Harper glided the luxurious car into place beside her little Jetta. As soon as she shifted into Park, Red opened his door.

"If you'll just be patient," she said, "I'll come around."

"Don't need your help."

He shifted to get out of the car while she rushed to help. He waved her off and stood on his own. He beamed at her as if he'd finished a marathon. "Told you I had it."

"The physical therapy's helping after all."

He harrumphed, as she'd known he would. He'd balked at the suggestion, but she and Derrick had insisted he at least give therapy a try. He was moving better and with less pain since he'd begun the twice-weekly sessions, but he'd never admit it.

She knew better than to press the point.

Inside, she settled him in a chair in the eat-in kitchen. "I have that leftover fettuccini we ordered yesterday, or I could make you a—"

"Pasta will work," he said.

She took out the creamy dish and spooned the leftovers into a pan. While it warmed, she fetched Red a bottle of yellow Gatorade, his favorite, unscrewed the top, and poured it into his glass. "Here you go."

He sipped the liquid, then leveled his blue-gray eyes on her. "Where's that grandson of mine?"

She pasted on a smile. "Derrick's been working hard lately." Working *and playing* hard, she knew. She cared for Derrick, but she wasn't impressed by how little time he made for his grandfather, his only living relative. At first, he'd driven up to Red's from his Baltimore condo every weekend to visit. But lately, things had changed. He'd quit visiting as often, and when he did, he seemed stressed. Worried.

Whatever it was, Harper saw no reason for him to neglect his grandfather. Maybe Derrick had only brought her here so he wouldn't feel as guilty about it.

Not that Harper had the right to judge. She hadn't spoken to her own parents in years. Hadn't spoken to her brothers, either. Sure, Dad had told her not to call, but she would someday. When things here were settled, when she knew the job would last. When she could handle their rejection.

"Works all the time, that boy," Red said.

She spooned helpings onto two plates and carried them to the table. "Maybe I should learn to cook fettuccini Alfredo."

Red smirked. "Stick to what you're good at."

She set the plates down and opened the silverware drawer. "You saying I'm a bad cook?"

"The worst." His lips twitched with the insult. "But you're the best nurse."

She set forks on the table and plopped into her chair. "That's because I have the best patient."

"Humph. Don't know about that." He held out his hand, and she took it. She'd gotten accustomed to the grace he said before every meal. He uttered a quick prayer, let go of her hand, and dug into his meal, flashing his bald head at her as he focused on getting the pasta to his mouth. Red had a point about her cooking. She'd tried, truly she had, but she hated it. Apparently it hated her, too. Anything beyond grilled cheese sandwiches and canned soup seemed to revolt at her incapable hands.

She was no cook. But caring for Red? That came as naturally as breathing. Maybe because she loved the old man so.

Harper felt so fortunate to be working for him, living in this lovely house. The thought from earlier returned—maybe God really did love her.

Could it be true? Estelle had been so sure.

And now Red. And the pastor at the church Red attended.

"What you thinking on, girl?"

"The pastor's message yesterday."

He wiped his mouth, nodding. "Good message. Got a question?"

She didn't have a question, not really. She just wasn't sure about it. "You believe all that? That we have to forgive because God forgave us first?"

"Course I do. Which part bothers you? The forgiving or the being forgiven?"

"Second part, I guess," she said. Because forgiveness for *all* her sins? All of them? Seemed too good to be true. When things seemed too good to be true, they usually were. Like this move to Maryland. Sure, the job was perfect, better than she'd ever imagined. But Derrick? She was starting to wonder if it was time to end the relationship. Not that he was doing anything wrong, certainly nothing she could put her finger on. He just seemed...tetchy lately. Short-tempered. When she'd asked about it, he acted as if she were the one with the problem.

More than that, she'd been very clear before she moved that she wasn't going to sleep with him until she was sure they would stay together, until she was sure he could be trusted. She'd also been clear that the move to Maryland had been about taking care of Red, not about making promises to Derrick. He'd agreed at the time.

But lately, he'd been pushing her. Not just to sleep with him, but also to make promises she wasn't ready to make. Promises about her love and devotion. Promises about their future. Between his making fewer trips to Red's house and the way he'd pushed her when he did come, she didn't know what to think.

Maybe she was too cautious. Maybe she'd been burned too

often. And maybe she needed, like Derrick had told her over and over, to trust him. He hadn't hurt her, hadn't lied to her. He'd gotten her this great job.

Frustration pulled like a too-tight jacket. She needed to be sure about Derrick, sooner rather than later. But so much of the time they spent together, Red was with them. How could their relationship progress if they didn't spend more time alone with one another? How could she learn to trust him when he was absent so often?

Because she wasn't sure about him, she wouldn't sleep with him, and she wouldn't make those promises. Not yet.

Which brought her back to the pastor's message the day before.

"And the first part," she said. "The part about how, if we forgive others, we don't let them off the hook."

"We let ourselves off the hook," Red said. "That's the part that stuck with me, too. We forgive for our sake, not anybody else's."

"Right." Harper needed to forgive Emmitt and Barry for what they'd done, for the crime that had landed all three of them in prison. Maybe if she could forgive them, she could trust Derrick. Maybe that's what was holding her back.

"The second part's more important." Red set down his fork and stared at her across the table. "The part about how God forgives all our sins. You get that part?"

She shrugged. "Seems too good to be true."

"That's God for you," he said. "Good, glorious, beautiful, perfect, and full of love for us."

"Why, though, when people are so messed up?"

One eyebrow lifted. "People, in general?" he asked. "Or someone in particular?"

"Fine. Why would He forgive me? You know my past. Why would God forgive what I've done?"

Red's smile lit his face. "He created you, didn't He? He knows all your frailties. His love is big enough for all your junk."

"I don't get it."

Red patted her hand. "You will. I believe soon, you will."

CHAPTER FIVE

Harper was scrolling through the website of the local college Friday afternoon when the front door opened.

"Who's that?" Red asked, as if she could see through walls and around corners. Not that there were many options. Most folks knocked.

She stood from her seat on the sofa. "I'll go check." She was halfway across the living room when Derrick stepped into the room. He saw her, and his face split into a huge smile.

"Surprise."

"What are you doing here?" She crossed the room, and he pulled her into a hug, then gave her a quick kiss.

"I took the afternoon off."

Red put down the footrest on his recliner and pushed himself to standing. "Great to see you, son."

The men hugged briefly. Then Red settled back in his seat, and Derrick sat on the sofa. "How you feeling, Gramps?"

"Couldn't be better," he said. "Got the best care a man could ask for."

Both men looked at her, and warmth rushed to her cheeks. "Can I get you anything? Iced tea?"

"Half-sugar tea, you mean?" Derrick asked.

"If I'd known you were coming," she said, "I'd have left the sugar out."

"Don't know why she needs so much," Red said. "She's sweet enough without it."

She ignored the remark and focused on Derrick. "I have Coke."

"Water's fine," he said.

"You hungry?"

"Depends. Did you cook?"

She forced a stern look. "Ha-ha."

He chuckled. "Not hungry. And I really can take care of myself."

She ignored him and went to the kitchen to get him a glass of water. When she returned, Red and Derrick were deep in conversation. She paused at the threshold, tuned out their words, and focused on the men.

They didn't look a bit alike. Derrick's features were more like Red's late wife's. Her photos were all over the house, and Harper could see the resemblance in the hazel eyes. She imagined when Red was a young man, he must have been built like Derrick was now. Not quite six feet, trim, healthy. Derrick had a full head of dark brown hair that he wore combed away from his face, which accentuated his widow's peak—or maybe it was a receding hairline. He played golf and tennis and worked out regularly, and he looked so professional and impressive in his dark suit. On weekends, he looked just as good in khakis and golf shirts. His wire-rim glasses only added to his charm.

Right now, he was leaning toward Red, nodding as the old man told a story, laughing with him. She loved how Red lit up when Derrick visited.

Too bad Derrick didn't come more often. So why was he here now?

He looked up and caught her eye. "Don't just stand there. Join us."

She stepped into the living room and handed him the ice water. "I didn't want to interrupt."

He focused on Red again. "I told you she was great, didn't I?"

"Gotta hand it to you," Red said. "You picked a winner."

She shook her head at their teasing.

Derrick focused on Red. "You think you can live without her for a couple of days?"

Based on Red's surprised expression, he didn't know what Derrick was talking about any more than she did.

"What's going on?" she asked.

"One of my clients has a summer house on Rehoboth Beach, and they're having a party tomorrow. They want us to come for the weekend."

A weekend on the beach. That sounded marvelous. And a weekend away, with Derrick? Maybe this would be a good opportunity to find out what was going on with him. See if the two of them could reconnect. They'd had a closer relationship when she'd lived in Vegas than they did now.

But what about Red?

She looked at the old man, then focused on Derrick. "I'm not sure I should leave him."

"Bah," Red said. "I survived without you for more'n eighty years." He picked up the photograph of his late wife and stared at it. "I got my memories of Bebe here to keep me company. I can manage two days."

"Yeah, but your medication, and—"

"Girl, I'm not a child. I can fend for myself for two days. You kids go, have a good time."

Derrick's smile only widened. "How would it make him feel if you refused now?"

What did Derrick expect from her? Promises she couldn't make? Commitments she wasn't ready for? Or a physical relationship she'd sworn she wouldn't give in to. She wiped sweaty hands on her jeans and held Derrick's gaze. "And what would the"—she cleared her throat and cut her gaze to Red—"*arrangements* be?"

Derrick's smile faded. "They have seven bedrooms. If they

don't have an extra place for me to sleep, I can stay at a hotel down the beach."

It was clear that hadn't been his intention. But he held her gaze, and that one eyebrow rose again. "Please?"

"Good Lord, girl," Red said. "I told you, I can fend for myself."

With Derrick's pleading and Red's cajoling, how could she refuse? A weekend at the beach sounded heavenly, and as long as Derrick was willing to keep his promise about giving her time, what was the downside?

She smiled at both the men now staring at her. "When do we leave?"

"As soon as you're ready."

CHAPTER SIX

Harper pulled her smallest bag from the closet. She could do nothing about its shabbiness, the splitting seam or the rickety wheel. With a sigh, she turned to study her wardrobe.

She'd need a dress for the party. Knowing Derrick's friends, she'd need something at least a little dressy. She didn't have a lot of options, but she found a pretty skirt and a peasant top that seemed suitable for a party on the beach. Derrick had bought both for her shortly after she'd moved. She added a pair of strappy sandals to go with that outfit. After throwing her bathing suit and cover-up in the bag, she added a couple pairs of shorts and a pair of patterned capris, a few of her nicer T-shirts, and her ugliest pajamas—just in case she was tempted to break her own rules.

She freshened her makeup, gathered her toiletries, and added them to the suitcase.

When the suitcase was zipped—no easy task considering the shape it was in—she opened her bedroom door to find Red sitting on the chair she'd put at the top of the stairs, a place for him to rest after climbing to the second floor.

She froze. "Are you all right?"

"Course." He glanced toward the back staircase, at the bottom of which Derrick was probably pacing, waiting for her. He lowered his voice. "I've been thinking… Can I talk to you for a second?"

She backed into her bedroom, and Red stepped just far enough inside to close the door. He hadn't been in her room since the day he'd showed her to it when she moved there, but this was his house, and he was practically family. "What's up?"

He rubbed his bald head. "Got the feeling you weren't excited about this trip."

"It'll be fun."

He studied her a moment. "Something tells me it won't."

Hadn't he just urged her to go? "What's that mean?"

He stared past her, out the window to the sunshiny day beyond. Took a deep breath and blew it out. Then, he focused on her. "I love my grandson. But… I don't know. I'm afraid…" He half-smiled. "Maybe I just don't want you to go."

She stepped toward him. "I can stay. If it makes you nervous—"

"Nothing like that." He waved her words away. "Just… Don't let Derrick talk you into anything. I know how you kids are these days, and I'm not judging. I'm just saying, that boy of mine, he doesn't have the best…" He seemed to falter, then shrugged. "Morals, I guess. His father didn't, either. Good man, my son, but he made a lot of mistakes. Derrick has, too. He's a decent kid, and I know he cares about you. But don't you let him talk you into anything you don't want to do."

That this man she'd only known for a couple of months would haul himself up the stairs to say this to her… Her eyes tingled, and she stepped closer. She set her hand over his where he leaned on her bureau. "If Derrick's half the man you are, any woman would be lucky to have him."

The man's cheeks reddened. "Just saying, you don't owe that boy nothing. He brought you out here for this job, but I hired you, I pay you, and I decide if you stay or go." His bushy eyebrows pushed up on his forehead. "You understand what I'm saying?"

"Thank you." She kissed his cheek and squeezed his hand. "I love you, too."

"Bah." His cheeks turned an even darker shade. He huffed out the door. The sweet, grouchy, beautiful old man. He'd meant every word, and so had she.

CHAPTER SEVEN

H arper had never been to the beach on the East Coast. Red's house wasn't far from Chesapeake Bay, but this was different.

While Derrick maneuvered his Mercedes toward the beach house that afternoon, cursing the traffic, Harper stared across the sand to the ocean beyond. The sky was blue, and the steel-gray water seemed to go on forever. The waves were high—higher than usual, Derrick said, thanks to a storm a few hundred miles south. It was predicted to head out to sea long before it reached the Delaware coast. Funny how the waters churned and battered the shore because of a storm she couldn't even see.

"Come on, buddy!" Derrick hammered the steering wheel when the car in front of them stopped for a yellow light. "At this rate, we'll never get there."

He was more keyed up than she'd ever seen him. He'd spent most of the bumper-to-bumper three-hour drive on the phone with clients. Because, apparently, stockbrokers didn't get to take time off, not even lazy Friday afternoons in July. When Derrick wasn't on the phone, he was yelling at other drivers.

She turned to him and smiled. "How can you be so grouchy? Look around. It's beautiful!" Her voice hitched on that last word, excitement and joy bubbling up and over. When was the last time she'd had a vacation? Gone anywhere fun?

Derrick glared at her, but the expression only lasted a moment. Then his lips drew tightly across his teeth. "You're right. Sorry. We're just late."

"Late for what?"

"Russell told me to be there by dinnertime, and it's"—he glanced at the clock on the dash—"nearly six-thirty."

"I'm sure he'll understand."

His plastic smile faded to a scowl. "I'm sure you *don't* understand. Russell is my biggest client. Not only that, but he's recommended me to a lot of his associates, and if this weekend goes well, he'll recommend me to more. I think his friend will be there this weekend. Constantine. The guy's loaded and swears his lineage goes back to Aphrodite." He smiled at that. "Or so goes the story he likes to tell. I've been trying to get his business for a couple of years. If I can impress him..." The promise of riches lay at the end of that unfinished sentence. But Derrick didn't smile at the thought of it. No, his lips tightened at the corners, and he focused on the road as they inched along.

There was that stress again. That worry. What was going on with him?

There was something he hadn't told her, something that mattered. Maybe this weekend, she'd get to the bottom of it.

One thing was sure. She'd need to do her best to impress this Russell guy and his buddy, Constantine.

Who traced his lineage back to a goddess.

No pressure there.

The phrase *delusions of grandeur* passed through her mind, but she pushed it away. She had to be charming and pleasant, which would be a feat in itself, more so if she were silently judging everyone.

As if she had the right to judge another living soul.

Despite Derrick's dire predictions, they arrived at the house ten minutes later. She wasn't sure what she'd expected. Derrick had told her the house had seven bedrooms, so she'd assumed it would be palatial, would have land and tended grounds and plenty of parking. All her assumptions had been wrong, though. She stared up at a three-story structure with a screened-in porch on the bottom floor and balconies on the upper two. The house was so close to its neighbors, there was barely room for a car between them, much less a garage. All the houses had been packed onto this beach like crackers in a sleeve. But the ones behind this didn't have views of the ocean. This one did, and for that the owners must have paid more than she'd earn in a lifetime.

Derrick found a parking spot, popped the trunk, and climbed out of the car. She snatched her purse from the backseat and joined him, inhaling the salty, briny scent of the Atlantic.

Funny how different this was from the beaches on the West Coast. The people were different here, too. Not all perfectly sculpted as they'd seemed in California. Not all blond and beautiful. They were normal people, her kind of people, and they were everywhere. Walking along the sidewalks in bikinis and T-shirts and flip-flops. Sitting side-by-side or standing in groups on porches and balconies, sipping adult beverages and laughing, grilling burgers and hot dogs, enjoying a perfect Friday afternoon in the summertime. A small family clad in dripping suits and gritty sand wandered past. They looked sunburned, exhausted, each holding a snack. The scent of fried dough and cinnamon had her stomach growling.

She turned when the trunk slammed. Derrick smiled at her, eyebrows up, and lifted their suitcases. "You ready?"

Could she pull this off? Pretend to be a normal person, someone who belonged among Derrick's high-society friends?

At least, if nothing else, she could always escape to the beach.

"Let's go."

Even with a suitcase in each hand, Derrick outpaced her so that she had to practically run to keep up.

At the door, Derrick set the suitcases down and knocked.

A moment later, a man answered. He was slender and tall and

looked to be in his early fifties, despite his nearly bald head. He had a strong chin, and though he wasn't physically imposing, he radiated power and confidence. He had piercing blue eyes that regarded Derrick with a look she couldn't discern before they focused on her.

He held out his hand. "Russell Caldworth. Harper, isn't it?"

She took it. "Pleasure to meet you."

"I've heard a lot about you."

She glanced at Derrick. "Good stuff, I hope."

"Every word." Russell turned to Derrick and shook his hand. "Great to see you again. Glad you made it. Traffic bad?"

"The worst."

Russell chuckled. "Friday at the beach. Apparently we weren't the only ones with this idea." He led the way through the living room. In the kitchen on the far side of the great room, a few women were chattering, slicing, stirring. Harper picked up the scent of garlic.

"My wife and some friends are fixing dinner. It'll be ready soon."

"Can I help?" Harper asked.

Derrick's laugh seemed forced. "Please, no. Don't let her cook."

Russell focused on her, eyebrows lifted. "Did you earn that remark?"

"Unfortunately, yes."

He smiled and continued through the living room. Beyond a wall of windows and sliding glass doors, Harper saw two men in the screened-in porch seated on wicker furniture, beer bottles in hand.

Russell climbed a staircase, and she and Derrick followed. Though the staircase went up another level, Russell stopped on the second floor, led them down a short hallway, and pushed open a door. "This'll be your room, Harper."

She stepped inside, barely glanced at the queen-size bed and, beyond it, an attached bath, then walked to the door that led to a balcony. She took in the beach and the gray waters of the Atlantic. "Wow."

Behind her, Russell said, "Derrick, are you staying here with her, or do you need another space?"

Harper tensed. She hoped Derrick would give the right answer.

"Uh," Derrick said. "Well, I was thinking—"

"Another space, then." Russell's tone left no room for argument.

She blew out a breath and turned. The older man winked at her.

"There's a kids' room upstairs that should accommodate you. I'm sorry we don't have another like this to offer, but if I know you, you won't sleep much, anyway."

"That'll be great. I'll be happy"—Derrick seemed far from it when he cut his gaze to her—"as long as Harper's comfortable."

Russell nodded toward the door, and Derrick stepped back into the hallway. "We'll eat in about an hour," Russell told her over his shoulder. "We're really casual tonight, so what you're wearing is fine. Come down whenever you're ready." With that, he closed the door.

Harper turned again to the view, then opened the slider and stepped outside.

The evening was perfect. Laughter and chatter from the men below joined the sound of the surf like a lovely serenade. A warm breeze blew her hair into her face, and she pushed it behind her ears.

The sun was setting behind the house, casting shadows on the beach and the few folks who lingered there. One couple strolled hand-in-hand along the boardwalk that seemed to stretch forever in both directions.

The ocean was breathtaking. Waves crashed against the sand, then slid back out, just like they'd done for thousands of years. Just like they'd do for thousands more. The thought made her feel small and insignificant.

Estelle's final words reverberated in her mind. Red's words, too. That God loved her. That despite all evidence to the contrary, despite the pile of mistakes she'd made, the sins she'd committed, she had a God who loved her.

Loved *her*.

It was inconceivable.

Yet, look at all He'd done. Brought her to this job and, through Derrick, to this amazing place.

Harper looked toward the endless blue sky. If God was there, she wanted to know Him. She wanted to believe. She imagined walking the beach, asking all her questions to the God who'd created all of this. If only she'd remembered her journal.

Laughter drifted up from downstairs and snapped her out of her musings. Derrick would expect her to go down and mingle, so that's what she'd do, despite her desire to stay here, to soak in this view. She was at the beach to have fun but also to help Derrick impress Russell and his friends.

Back in her room, she opened her bag, grabbed her toiletries, and carried them to the attached bathroom. After she'd brushed her hair and applied some makeup, she surveyed her reflection. Before they'd left Red's house, she'd put on white capris with a teal sleeveless blouse that accentuated the blue of her eyes. Russell had said this outfit would do, so she wouldn't change. She was pretty, but she'd long since given up the belief that her looks were a blessing. Her looks had only led to trouble.

She'd trade all her beauty to get back those wasted years. But that deal wasn't on the table tonight and never would be.

CHAPTER EIGHT

H arper opened her bedroom door and listened. She heard women's voices, but no men's, which meant Derrick was either outside or still in his bedroom. Which meant she had to go downstairs and face a bunch of women she'd never met before, all by herself.

Which wasn't uncomfortable at all.

Right.

She stepped out of her room and closed the door behind her. Then she went down the stairs, resisting the urge to tiptoe.

The sound of women chattering mingled with the beeping of a timer, the humming of a vent fan.

At the bottom of the stairs, Harper peered beyond the long dining room table, which had been set to seat ten, to the screened-in porch, where Derrick was sitting on the arm of a chair. He held a brown beer bottle in one hand, a chip in the other. The other men held drinks, too, and talked. Russell was reclining, watching with those piercing eyes. She barely knew the older man, but after the way he'd handled Derrick upstairs, she liked him.

She debated for only a moment, then pasted on a smile and walked around the corner toward the kitchen.

The conversation came to an abrupt halt.

"You must be Harper." A fifty-something blonde with a short, relaxed haircut crossed the space, wearing an inviting smile. Over capris and a T-shirt, she wore an apron that read *I'm still hot. It just comes in flashes now.* She took both of Harper's hands in hers and squeezed. "It's such a pleasure to meet you. I'm Russell's wife, Betts."

With that wide smile and those joyful eyes, this woman seemed genuinely delighted. "Nice to meet you."

"I'm so sorry I didn't greet you at the door. I was in a critical moment with the bruschetta toast."

Another woman stepped beside Betts. Her hair was also blond, though the dye-job wasn't as professional, nor the haircut. "You know how finicky bruschetta toast can be."

Harper's chuckle surprised her. "I'm not even sure I know what bruschetta toast is."

Both women feigned gasps.

"We'll need to educate you!" Betts nodded toward the woman beside her. "This is my dear friend, Kitty Williams. She goes with Keith, who's outside."

Kitty shook Harper's hand. "Glad you could join us."

Harper nodded, focused on Betts again. "I appreciate the invitation."

Betts waved the thank-you off and stepped to the side. Harper focused on the other woman in the room, a thin, perfectly polished brunette with a plastic smile.

Betts said, "And this is Marjorie Slater."

Marjorie's smile tightened. She wore a black sleeveless turtle-neck—which set off a long strand of pearls perfectly—over black slacks and black sandals that had two-inch heels. Even with the extra height, Marjorie didn't stand more than five-four, yet she still managed, somehow, to look down her nose at Harper. "Lovely to meet you, Harper... What's your last name?"

"Cloud."

Marjorie glanced at the others, then back at Harper. "What an unusual name. Where did it come from?"

Harper wasn't sure how to answer that and was saved when Betts interrupted. "It came from her father, I assume." She turned to Harper. "Unless it's an ex's name."

"No ex—"

"Of course she's not divorced," Marjorie snapped. "Nobody would *choose* to keep Cloud as a last name."

Kitty's laugh was forced, and she focused on Harper. "Don't mind her. She's had a rough day."

Marjorie sipped from the red liquid in her martini glass. "And not nearly enough alcohol."

Silence settled among the women until Betts sighed and returned to the counter where she'd been working. "Kitty, get Harper a drink, would you?"

"Sure!" She turned to Harper. "We have beer, wine, and Marjorie made up a pitcher of cosmopolitans." She cut her gaze to the brunette. "Which I'm sure she wouldn't mind sharing."

"No, thank you," Harper said. "Just water for me."

Kitty's eyebrows lifted.

Marjorie uttered a little *pfft*.

Betts said, "Kitty, get the girl a glass of water. She's had a long drive. Then, could you finish up with that salad?"

Kitty jumped to action. Betts was stirring some kind of cream sauce on the stove.

Marjorie leaned against the counter and sipped her cosmo. When their gazes met, the woman gave her a saccharin smile.

She'd known her five minutes, and clearly the woman hated her.

The kitchen had been remodeled with granite countertops and had fresh paint on the cabinets, but it was no designer space. Just a normal kitchen to fix normal meals, which matched the kind woman currently preparing their dinner.

Dishes and pots and pans and various food items covered the counters. "Can I do anything to help?"

Betts turned to her with another big smile—the woman seemed as happy as anyone Harper had ever known—and nodded to a cookie sheet where slices of toast covered with some sort of tomato mixture were lined like soldiers. "You can transfer the bruschetta to a serving dish, if you don't mind."

"The serving dishes are where?"

Betts focused beyond Harper, and Harper turned to see Marjorie glaring at her back.

Betts said to Marjorie, "Grab her that blue dish from the cabinet, would you?"

Marjorie slid a pretty blue platter from the glass-fronted cabinet, handed it to Harper, and then settled back against the counter.

Harper pulled a spatula from a jar of utensils on the counter and shifted the little pieces of toast to the plate.

Kitty snatched one and took a bite. "Seriously, you should try it."

Betts said, "Go ahead."

Harper took one and bit into it. She tasted toast, tomatoes, garlic, basil, olive oil, and a sprinkling of some sort of white cheese. "This is delicious."

When she was halfway through her third and, sadly, last bite, Marjorie said, "So what do you do?"

Harper swallowed quickly, trying not to choke on her food. She sipped her water and met the woman's cold gaze. "I'm a private nurse. I care for Derrick's grandfather."

Marjorie's smirk seemed satisfied, though Harper had no idea why.

"A nurse!" Kitty sounded downright jubilant at the news. "I'm a doctor."

Harper faced her over the huge bowl of salad Kitty was tossing. "What's your specialty?"

"Pediatrics."

"You like your job?"

"Mostly, I love it. I only work part-time right now, so I can be home with my kids." She carried the salad to the dining room table around the corner. When she returned, she said, "But pediatrics is hard. Children aren't supposed to get sick."

Betts said, "It's so sad sometimes."

Harper turned to her. "You work there, too?"

"I'm just a volunteer at the hospital," Betts said. "I hold the babies and play with the kids."

"What a wonderful way to help," Harper said. "I bet you're universally loved."

Betts shrugged, and Kitty said, "She is. And you focus on geriatric patients?"

"I was working at a nursing home when Derrick and I met. I've always felt so comfortable with older folks. I can't imagine doing anything else."

"But it's sad, too," Kitty said. "In a nursing home, there's never a happy ending."

Harper shrugged. "I don't know. Death is a step in the natural order of things, isn't it? I lost a patient, a dear friend, right before I moved. She never talked about death, just about going home. I love that sentiment."

"If you know God," Betts said, "it's not just sentiment. It's truth."

Kitty's smile was indulgent before she turned back to Harper. "And Derrick's grandfather? Is he a good patient?"

Harper chuckled. "He's not always a *patient* patient, but he's a kind, sweet man. I've never had a better job."

Behind her, Marjorie *hmm'ed*. Harper made sure her smile was in place when she turned to face her. "And what do you do?"

"Nothing so *important* as what you do."

Harper was amazed at the woman's ability to make the word *important* sound like an insult.

Marjorie continued. "I work for a fashion designer in Manhattan."

"Oh. Sounds like a fun job."

"Fun." She sipped her drink. "Loads."

Betts poured a huge pot of pasta over a colander in the sink. "Get the guys, would you, Kitty? It's time to eat."

"Constantine isn't here yet." Marjorie's voice held more animation than it had yet. "Shouldn't we wait?"

Betts glanced at the clock. "It's seven-thirty. If he gets here, he gets here. I'm not waiting any longer."

Marjorie's tight lips told Harper what she thought of that.

Kitty passed the dining room table and opened the slider. "Soup's on."

The men walked into the house carrying their drinks and their conversation.

Derrick crossed to her side, took her hand, and leaned in. "Having fun?"

"Sure. They're nice." Her gaze cut to Marjorie, but Derrick didn't notice.

Harper turned to Betts, who was mixing cream sauce into pasta. "What can I do?"

Betts got her husband's attention. "Russell, make sure Harper meets everyone."

He nodded to his wife, then stood beside Harper. The two men she hadn't met were deep in conversation when Russell led her to them and interrupted. "Gentlemen, this is Harper Cloud."

Both men turned to her. One had longish brown hair, brown eyes, and dark skin. He was older and barely cracked a smile. "Keith Williams."

Kitty's husband. He couldn't be more different from the friendly woman Harper had met.

Russell said, "Keith's a police detective in Baltimore."

The word *police* had her stomach dropping, but only a little. She had nothing to fear from this man. She'd not so much as rolled a stop sign since she'd gotten out of prison. "Nice to meet you."

"You, too." His voice was gruff, and as soon as he'd spoken, his attention shifted elsewhere.

Russell turned to the other man. "And this is Marjorie's husband, Carter Slater."

Carter's gray eyes met her gaze with an intensity that made her want to step back. He took her hand in his, then covered it with his other hand. He moved closer, too close. "It's a great pleasure to meet you, Harper Cloud."

Adrenaline pumped into her veins as if he'd flipped a switch.

"Careful, Slater." Derrick's voice, right beside her, held a hint of warning beneath the forced chuckle. "She's spoken for."

Carter held her gaze a moment longer, then dropped her hands. "Just getting to know our new friend."

She flushed, and this time, she did step back. Marjorie glared at her from the far side of the room.

Great. They hadn't even eaten dinner yet, and she'd cemented her status as the enemy. Wouldn't this be fun?

CHAPTER NINE

The food was passed around the table. Fettuccini with a seafood cream sauce, angel-hair with a meat sauce, bruschetta, salad, and various side dishes. Harper loaded her plate, ravenous after the long day.

"Must be nice to be able to eat such rich and fattening foods." Marjorie, sitting on the other side of the table, eyed Harper's plate with disdain. "I can't imagine."

Harper snatched a couple of olives off the antipasto plate before she handed it to Carter. "It is, actually. I can eat whatever I want and never gain a pound."

At the look Marjorie gave her, she wondered if the woman knew how to do anything but glare.

Two seats down from Harper, Kitty laughed. "Every woman's dream!"

Betts added, "Men think our dream is to find Prince Charming. But no. It's calorie-free food."

Harper, Kitty, and Betts shared a laugh. Marjorie's lips tipped up in a feeble attempt before she helped herself to a bird-sized portion of angel-hair pasta.

Carter, who'd snatched the seat beside Harper, leaned in. "Whatever you're eating or not eating, it's working."

Harper shifted her attention to Derrick, sitting opposite her, hoping for some support. But he was focused on Russell.

Derrick asked, "How's business been? I read in the *Wall Street Journal* about that big merger—"

"Let's not talk shop tonight." Russell set the bowl of seafood pasta in the center of the table. He leaned over to Betts and kissed her on the cheek. "Looks delicious, babe."

She beamed at him. "I hope it tastes good."

They dug into their meals, and for a few moments, the only sounds were the scrape of silverware and the appreciative *mmms* of the diners.

"Wow." Keith lifted his fork, which was piled with pasta and tomato sauce. "This is awesome."

"Thank you," Betts said. "It's Russell's mother's recipe."

"Good cook, your mother?" Harper asked.

"Second best." Russell smiled at his wife, who blushed. They acted like newlyweds. Harper was about to ask how long they'd been married when a knock sounded at the door a moment before it opened.

A man stepped into the room. He was short, heavy-set, and had white hair and a white beard. He wore a sport coat over a polo shirt and slacks.

All the men stood. "Constantine," Russell said. "Glad you could make it."

Constantine surveyed the dinner table, and his eyes narrowed the tiniest bit. "I see you waited for me."

Russell just laughed. "Betts's house, Betts's rules."

Betts stood and produced a smile, though it was tight on the corners. "And Betts was hungry. Grab a seat."

Only when Constantine headed toward the table did Harper notice there was a woman behind him. She couldn't have been more than twenty-five. Blond, blue-eyed, slight, and beautiful.

Russell must've just noticed her, too. He crossed the room, and Betts followed. Russell held out his hand. "I'm Russell Caldworth. This is my wife, Betts. Welcome."

The woman glanced at Constantine before shaking Russell's hand. "Hi. I'm Jenny."

Russell introduced her to everyone, then introduced Constantine to Keith, Kitty, Derrick, and Harper, while Betts set another place at the table. The man barely nodded at any of them. He turned to the girl. "Come in and sit."

Jenny followed Constantine to the table.

And that's exactly what it was—obedience. In fact, except for Russell and Betts, everyone in the room seemed to fawn over Constantine. It wasn't shocking, really. The man emanated strength and power and authority. But did he wield those over this tiny, cowering woman?

Constantine sat at the end of the table, though Jenny hadn't reached her seat yet, the empty chair beside Harper. The rest of the men, Derrick included, waited until Jenny and Betts sat before they resumed their seats.

When the food had been passed to the new guests, Harper leaned toward Jenny. "I'm Harper. In case you missed it."

Her gaze flicked to Constantine, then to her plate. Then, for an instant, they focused on Harper. "Nice to meet you."

Constantine dominated the conversation, telling them about his latest business ventures, but Harper barely listened. She ate her dinner, tried to ignore Carter, who occasionally whispered comments in her ear that made her skin crawl, and focused on Jenny. Something about her didn't sit well. Harper had seen that vacant look in people's eyes before. Jenny reminded her of so many women she'd known back in Vegas, woman who'd latched on to some man thinking they'd hit the jackpot only to discover they themselves had been the prize. Women who'd gotten stuck with horrid men in horrid relationships and didn't have the courage to break free. Harper had seen that expression in the mirror. She knew it well.

Harper didn't know much about the world of finance and big business. But women being cowed and used? Unfortunately, that was a world she knew very well. She'd been there, and she'd met a lot of women who'd been there. If she'd come out of prison with nothing else, she'd come out with the determination to help women who were trapped in relationships with cruel men. She didn't know if Jenny was in that category, but she intended to find out and, if she could, to help.

Derrick caught her eye across the table. She could see the need there. The need for her to help him schmooze Constantine. She didn't think she'd be helping Derrick much tonight. Maybe if he knew what she did, he'd understand.

Something told her he wouldn't.

CHAPTER TEN

Constantine regaled them with stories like a king with his court. Harper couldn't deny the man was compelling. Marjorie even forgot to give Harper hate-filled glances when he was talking. Unfortunately, Carter didn't forget about Harper. Instead, when Constantine's stories alluded to the many women he'd known, Carter whispered comments under his breath that only Harper could hear, comments that had her hands clenching beneath the table. She said nothing in return, refusing to acknowledge his presence, though even if she could have pretended not to hear, his beer-and-garlic scented breath was impossible to ignore.

She glanced at Derrick a few times, hoping for some help, at least an encouraging smile, but Derrick, like Kitty, Keith, and Marjorie, had fallen under Constantine's spell.

Not Russell and Betts, though. They didn't interrupt him or try to steer the conversation elsewhere, but they shared the occasional lifted eyebrow or quiet laugh as though witnessing the scene as spectators, not participants.

Jenny barely glanced up from her plate.

Finally, when the serving dishes had been emptied of pasta, when the forks had been put down and Constantine had paused for a breath, Betts stood. "Anybody want a cup of coffee with dessert?"

When nobody but Harper took her up on that offer, Betts said, "Or another drink?"

Russell stood beside his wife, kissed her cheek, and said, "I'll manage the drinks. You get the pie."

"Who can possibly eat pie after such a heavy meal?" Marjorie spoke to the table but gave Harper a pointed look.

"I'd love some." Harper stood and began gathering dinner dishes.

Kitty helped, too. "Maybe if you moved more and drank less, Marjorie, you could eat dessert."

"Now, Kitty," Betts said, "I don't need anybody's help. Marjorie's our guest."

Kitty met Harper's gaze and rolled her eyes. For the first time since they'd sat for dinner, Harper felt a glimmer of amusement. When she reached for Jenny's plate, she smiled at her. "Want to join us?"

Jenny's gaze cut to Constantine. His nod was tiny, nearly imperceptible. Jenny pushed back her chair and took his plate.

They headed for the kitchen and started scraping dishes. Jenny went to the sink and ran the water.

"Oh, honey," Betts said. "I'll do the dishes if you'll just help clear the table."

Jenny's pale cheeks reddened just a bit. "I'll just wash the pots and pans, if you don't mind."

Betts regarded her with kind eyes, then snatched her apron off the counter. "Wear this so you don't get your pretty outfit dirty."

Jenny slid it on and settled in with sudsy water and a sponge.

Harper returned to the dining room to gather more dirty dishes.

"I can't imagine why you don't hire help for these gatherings." Constantine's remark was directed at Russell, who was carrying a few bottles of beer to the table. "I'm sure your wife would appreciate it."

Russell laughed. "You know Betts better than that." He looked at his wife, who was halfway to the kitchen with an empty platter in each hand. "I offered, believe me."

"My house, my rules." She winked at her husband and disappeared around the corner.

Harper snatched the remaining dirty dishes from the table.

"Her house?" Derrick took the offered beer, eyebrows lifted. "Did you give it to her?"

"Not even close, my friend," Russell said. "Unlike me, Betts came from wealth. This was their family's beach home when she was growing up. Her parents gave it to her when they relocated to Florida."

"Russell married up, to say the least." Constantine's words seemed laced with indulgence, superiority.

If Russell noticed, he didn't let on. "I married up in every conceivable way."

From the kitchen, Betts said, "And don't you forget it!" Then she rounded the corner and kissed his cheek. "And so did I." To everyone else, she said, "More water? Constantine, you need some Scotch?"

He nodded, and Russell headed toward the wet bar and poured the drink.

Harper took the remaining dishes to the kitchen. She'd never seen such a strong bond between a married couple as the one Russell and Betts shared. Harper's parents loved each other, but they'd never been quite so *in* love.

Though Betts had been focused on everyone at the table, her focus had always, first, been on Russell. And he'd been the same way.

So unlike Derrick, who'd not only not sat beside her but who'd barely looked at her all night. Derrick had been too busy sucking up to Russell and Constantine to pay any attention to her. Did he have any idea how he looked to outsiders? How desperate he seemed?

Desperate.

That was the word, the only word to describe what had changed with him in the previous few weeks. Now that she thought about it, it was crystal clear. It was the reason he'd barely spared her a glance all night, apparently hadn't even noticed how Carter had come on to her. The realization had her stomach dropping for the second time that evening. Because desperate men couldn't be trusted.

She'd learned that the hard way.

"Would you see who wants pie?" Betts asked.

"Sure." Harper pushed her worries about Derrick aside and returned to the dining room.

When everyone who wanted a slice of Bett's apparently famous cherry pie had some—that was to say, everyone except Marjorie and Jenny, who was still in the kitchen—Harper poured herself a cup of decaf and took her seat. She'd offered to help Jenny, but the girl shooed her away. She seemed in no hurry to return to the dining room.

Carter leaned close and whispered in her ear. "What's this I hear?"

She'd had it with his whispered remarks. Whatever Derrick's issue was, it wasn't her problem. She didn't have to put up with these comments from Carter or anybody. She turned to face him, let her voice rise. "What did you hear, Carter?"

The chattering at the table stopped. She felt their gazes on her, but she didn't break eye contact with the jerk.

His face flushed, and his smile got tight at the corners. He glanced at Marjorie, and Harper followed the gaze. The woman was glaring at them both.

Harper didn't have to put up with that, either. She ignored her.

"What's this?" Derrick's eyes narrowed as if he'd just realized what was going on.

"I hear you two are sleeping in separate bedrooms." Carter said it with a hint of humor and an undertone of spite.

Marjorie said, "Oh, for the love of—"

"What about it?" Derrick's face flushed, and his gaze flicked to Constantine and back to Carter.

"Just thought it was curious."

Russell's hand clamped down on Carter's shoulder. "Doesn't seem like that's any of your business, my friend." He focused on Marjorie. "Are you two planning anything special for your anniversary? That's coming up, right?"

"Five glorious years in September." Her expression said her marriage had been anything but, and Harper's animosity toward the woman shifted to sympathy. Who could blame her with a husband like Carter? "We were considering Florence."

"Wonderful choice," Betts said.

Harper focused on Marjorie. "Have you been there before?"

The woman blinked, focused on her, seemed to forget to scowl. In fact, she looked wistful. "When I was a little girl, my father took me. I've always wanted to go back."

Harper was about to ask a follow-up question when Constantine cleared his throat. "Yes, Florence is lovely, all that art. Have you ever been to Mykonos?" And he launched into stories of Greece, which he called his homeland, though based on his accent, he'd been born and raised in New York.

Finally, dessert was finished, the dishes cleared, and Constantine seemed to run out of stories. He pushed back in his chair and stood. "Let's play cards, shall we?"

CHAPTER ELEVEN

Harper poured herself another cup of decaf and glanced at Derrick, who stood beside Constantine at the wet bar, pouring two glasses of Scotch.

Just what Derrick needed—to get a little drunker, suck up a little more.

This was not the man she'd met in Vegas.

She'd come on this weekend away because she'd wanted to get to know him better. So far, she didn't like what she saw.

Harper joined the rest of the ladies on the screened-in porch. After the cool of the air conditioning, the warm muggy air wrapped around her like a blanket. Hot coffee had been a bad idea.

A white wicker sofa and a couple of matching chairs were arranged to form a seating area. Betts, Kitty, and Marjorie were on the sofa. Jenny chose one of the chairs, so Harper settled into the other and stared at the surf beyond the boardwalk. "It's beautiful."

"It's my happy place," Betts said. "I have a lot of good memories in this house."

"And you're making a lot more," Kitty said. "Are you missing your kids tonight?"

Betts smiled. "A little, but they're having fun with my folks in Florida. They'll be back next week."

"How old are they?" Harper asked.

Harper learned about Betts and Russell's two teenagers, then about Kitty and Keith's three kids—all under four. Apparently, Marjorie and Carter didn't have any children, though whether by choice or not, she didn't know.

"Do you want children?" Betts asked Harper. "Assuming you find the right man." She laughed and added, "Not that Derrick isn't the right man. That's not what I meant."

Harper smiled. "I knew what you meant. Yeah, someday, I'd love to have kids. I never thought I'd want them, but you reach a certain age—"

"What are you," Marjorie asked, "twenty-one?"

If only she could be that young again. If only she could go back and make better choices and change the previous seven years. "I'm twenty-eight."

"Really?" Kitty said. "You're just two years younger than I am." She focused on Marjorie. "Take a good look, honey." She pointed back and forth between Harper and herself. "This is what kids'll do to you." She regarded Harper again and added, "Not that I ever looked like that."

Harper waved off the comment. "Don't be silly. You're beautiful."

Kitty looked at Betts and feigned a sympathetic tone. "So young to be losing her eyesight."

Betts bumped Kitty's shoulder. "You're the only person who thinks you're not beautiful."

"These pregnancy pounds—"

"Only add to it." Betts turned to Jenny. "And what about you? Do you want kids someday?"

The young woman shrugged and glanced inside. "Probably not."

"You don't want them," Betts said, "or you don't think you'll have them?"

"Constantine has children from his first wife. He doesn't want more."

Betts's smile faded. "But what do *you* want?"

Jenny swallowed, shrugged. "I don't know."

"How long have you two been together?" Kitty asked.

"A few years."

Betts's eyebrows disappeared behind her blond bangs. "Years? I had no idea."

Jenny looked toward the surf. "I prefer to stay at home when he travels. He's always so busy."

"Pfft!" Marjorie slammed her glass on the table. "He treats you like dirt."

Jenny's face paled, and she glanced through the screen toward the men inside. As if Constantine paid her any attention at all. The men had gathered around the smaller kitchen table and were in the middle of a game of poker.

"My dear friend." Betts reached across Kitty and patted Marjorie's leg. "I'm not sure you ought to be throwing stones." She pulled her hand away and focused on Jenny again. "I'd love to hear your story."

Marjorie said nothing, just studied Jenny.

The woman seemed to wilt under their gazes.

Harper cleared her throat and worked up her courage. Being candid was not her strong suit. "I've been there."

All the gazes turned to her.

"Dated a guy back in..." She swallowed. Decided not to share that much. "Before I met Derrick. He started out being so nice to me, treated me like gold—for the first few months. After that, I was window dressing. Brought along because I looked good on his arm." Had she just complimented herself? How ridiculous she must look. But it was true, so she continued. "Looks are liars, let me tell you. I was a mess. After a while, you start believing you're equal to the way you're being treated. As if you're a reflection of everyone else's opinion of you. He treated me like dirt until I believed I was dirt."

Jenny leaned forward. That interest was enough to keep Harper talking.

"Then one day, I'd had enough. I broke up with him."

"What happened?" Jenny asked.

"It's taken me a long time to stop seeing dirt in the mirror." She reached across the space to Jenny and squeezed her hand, then let it go. "Dumping the guy was the first step. I wish I'd had some good friends before I did it. I ended up with another guy who treated me exactly the same, and the cycle started all over again."

"Not that it's any of my business," Marjorie asked, "but is that the reason for the separate bedrooms?"

The question surprised her, but not as much as the person who'd asked it. "That's exactly the reason. I don't trust men very easily. I doubt I'll ever trust a man again. Right now, I need to know I'm not some guy's hobby or decoration. A little something to brag about when people aren't impressed with his new car or new watch. I'm not just the dirt clinging to some man's shoes."

"Amen." Betts lifted her water glass in a sort of salute. "You're smart to wait, to make sure it's real."

"How will you know if he can be trusted?" Marjorie asked. "How can anybody ever know?"

If Harper had the answer to that, she'd have found Mr. Right long before—and skimmed over all those Mr. Wrongs. Clearly, Marjorie, too, had trusted the wrong man. She'd been married for five years to a man who'd flirt with another woman right under her nose. A man who'd rub her face in it.

Betts sighed. "Maybe I just got lucky."

"You did," Marjorie said.

"I did, too," Kitty said. "Keith's a good guy. He's never strayed. He's made some stupid decisions." A shadow crossed her face. "But I know he loves me and the kids."

Betts said, "He does. The rest of it, he'll get figured out."

Apparently Betts knew the story, whatever it was.

The women were quiet a moment as a few young men wandered down the boardwalk, laughing and ribbing each other. Their voices faded until only the sound of the surf and the muted noise of the men inside filled the silence.

An enjoyable moment, not just because of the beach and the

women who surrounded her, but because she realized she didn't feel nervous. Didn't feel like somebody was watching her. Even at Red's house, she sometimes got that prickly feeling on her arms. That's how she knew she was crazy. What kind of stalker would follow her across the country?

None. Obviously.

But she felt safe tonight. Maybe the fear was wearing off. Maybe that's all it had ever been.

The man in the alley back in Vegas must have just seen her and followed. Bad luck on her part, nothing more.

"I think..." It was Jenny who spoke, and the rest of the women turned to her.

Harper leaned in, willed her to continue.

Jenny swallowed. "I think maybe I've trusted the wrong man."

Betts stood, crossed the small porch, and crouched beside Jenny's chair. "I've known Constantine since he and Russell were at school together. They've been friends for thirty years. Constantine is a great businessman. He used to be a good man. But the wealth, the success... He's changed. And not for the better." She patted the young woman's knee. "I don't say this to hurt you, Jenny, but to help, okay?"

"Okay."

"You say you've been with him for years?" At Jenny's nod, Betts continued. "We've seen him many times in the last few years. He's never without a woman. And he's never mentioned your name."

Jenny's expression didn't change except for the tears that filled her eyes. She opened her mouth, then closed it again.

"Where does your family live?" Harper asked.

"I'm from Missouri."

"Go home," Harper said. "That's what I did wrong. I was too proud to go home after I dumped loser number one. If I had..." If she had, everything would have been different.

Jenny nodded, tried a smile. "I could do that."

Could. The telltale word. "You need money?" Not that Harper had it to give, but she'd scrape it up if she had to. "For a plane ticket?"

But Jenny wiped her eyes, sat straighter. "I'm okay."

"Whatever you need," Betts said. "It's yours."

"Constantine gives me everything I need." She smiled at Betts. "I'll think about what you said."

She'd think about it, but she wouldn't leave. Because sometimes, the evil you shared a bed with was better than the great alone. Harper understood the lie. She'd lived it.

Marjorie stared at the surf. It seemed she'd allowed herself to believe the same thing. That the familiar trumped the unknown.

Neither of them understood. When you were alone, when you didn't trust anybody, then nobody could hurt you.

CHAPTER TWELVE

I t was nearly midnight. With all the alcohol, Marjorie turned maudlin, Jenny got quieter, and Kitty cracked jokes that became stupider—and somehow funnier—by the minute. Betts, who'd hardly had a drink all night, observed the scene with patient indulgence, like a fond parent.

Harper bid them all good-night. Inside, she crossed the great room to the kitchen table, where the men were still engaged in their poker game. Constantine and Carter had piles of chips in front of them. Derrick looked to be nearly out. His scowl told Harper as much as the lack of chips did. She stopped beside his chair and bent to kiss his cheek. "I'm going to bed."

He barely glanced at her. "Fine. Good night."

She stepped back, surprised at his rudeness.

His expression shifted from irritated to apologetic. "I'm sorry. You okay?"

"She's fine." Carter's words were slurred and slushy. "More than fine."

Derrick glared at the man, started to push back in his seat. "You need to learn to keep your mouth shut."

Russell's hand clamped down on Derrick's shoulder, but he glared at Carter. "Maybe it's time for you to go to bed."

"No." Derrick scooted back to the table. "He's not going to bed until he gives me a chance to win my money back."

Harper stood another moment, then realized Derrick had forgotten she was there. Forgotten he'd been about to defend her, take up for her. Not that she wanted anyone to fight, but to see that he cared about her might have been nice. Right now, all he cared about was winning back his money.

Gambling. She'd never understood the allure of it. Money was hard to come by and too easy to lose. She'd seen a lot of people in Las Vegas who'd been destroyed because of gambling.

She headed for the stairs. The heat of someone's gaze warmed her. Maybe Derrick felt a twinge of remorse for his rudeness. But when she turned to look, it was Carter whose leer had followed her across the room.

She climbed the stairs quickly. Once she got to her bedroom, she closed the door and turned the lock. Then she tested it.

The door pulled open.

She tried again, but though the lock engaged, the door didn't close completely, rendering the lock useless.

Fear rose like flames, but she tamped it down. Nobody was out to get her. Carter wouldn't dare come into her room uninvited, not with his wife under the same roof. Not after Harper had shut him down at dinner.

She wouldn't let fear keep her from sleep. So the door didn't lock. So what? She was safe here.

She'd spent far too much of her life living in fear. Besides, nobody could hurt her. She'd learned in prison how to defend herself—or at least how to make enough noise to alert the guards.

She'd be fine.

Ten minutes later, she'd scrubbed off the makeup and pulled on the yellow pajamas she'd had since high school. They had tiny pink bunnies all over and were frayed at the hems. Happy to be alone after the long day, she slipped beneath the sheets, wishing she could open the patio door and listen to the surf. But the air conditioner was humming, and she didn't want to warm up her cool room.

She didn't know how long she'd slept when she woke. The house was quiet now, no murmurs from the party downstairs. She opened her eyes. What had woken her?

She heard a creak, saw through the darkness as the door inched open. She couldn't see who it was, but she had her suspicions.

Carter. The creep.

Harper flashed back to night after night of sleeping with one eye open. Most of her cellmates had been scary but not terribly dangerous. But she'd had one she hadn't trusted. Harper had learned to be ready.

She should have grabbed her pepper spray and her little keychain knife. Stupid. Hadn't she learned better?

She stayed still, clenched her hands into fists. Waited for him to get close enough. She'd hit him, hard, and then she'd scream. In prison, no guards would have cared. But in this house, she'd get everyone's attention.

The man inched across the hardwood floor to the far side of the bed, then pulled back the covers.

"Don't even think about it." Her words reverberated in the silence. The man froze.

"I thought you were sleeping."

"Derrick?"

A pause, then, "Who else would it be?" His words were barely a whisper.

She matched the volume. "I thought..." She sat up and faced him where he stood on the far side of the bed. The moonlight beyond the gauzy curtains in front of the sliding door offered just enough to make out his silhouette.

"You thought what?"

She shook off the fear, unclenched her fists. "Nothing. What are you doing?"

He sat heavily on the bed and stared toward the glass. "Rough night. I just thought... I needed to be with you."

She shifted to face his back and rested her palm there. "Did something happen?"

"I lost. Big time."

She patted his shoulder. "That's not the end of the world, is it?"

His laugh was short and filled with bitterness. "You don't understand."

"Explain it to me, then."

He said nothing, just stared toward the sliders.

"It's okay," she said. "You can tell me about it tomorrow. Why don't you go on to bed, sleep it off?"

He shifted so that he was facing her, his bare feet on the bed with the rest of him. He leaned on one arm, pulled her against his chest with the other. "I need you, Harper." He leaned in and kissed her. He tasted like booze.

She knew what he *needed*, and it had nothing to do with her. Any warm female body could have satisfied that need. She rested her palms against his chest and pushed. "No. You're drunk, and I'm not interested."

He pulled her close again, nestled his face against her neck. Kissed the skin there. "Don't you understand? You're the only one who can save me."

She waited for some twinge of desire, but all she felt was annoyance. Maybe a little fear. She scooted away, tossed the covers back, and slipped out of the bed. "Save you from what?"

"From... from myself." He leaned toward her, held out his hand. "Please, let me hold you."

She flipped on the light.

They both blinked in the sudden brightness. Derrick seemed to shrink from it.

"This isn't going to happen tonight," she said.

"I'm not... We don't have to do anything. Just, can I please stay with you? I don't want to be alone."

Right. He'd just lie there and let her sleep? Even if he did manage to keep his hands to himself—which she highly doubted—she'd never be able to relax with him there.

But he looked so sad, so lost.

He needed her. She understood that need, that bone-deep desire to be held, to be loved. It wasn't sex he needed but affection. This man who'd lost both his parents, who had no siblings, whose only relative was an octogenarian grandfather.

Derrick felt alone. Lonely. He needed her.

She was being selfish.

"Please." His arm was still stretched toward her.

She started to reach for him, then let her arm drop while the words he'd uttered earlier came back. *You're the only one who can save me.* What did he need to be saved from, and why would he think she could do it?

She flashed back to those sweet counselors who'd visited the prison. They'd taught her that her biggest addiction wasn't substances, but people. Her need to love and be loved. She remembered the pattern they'd pointed out and how she'd spent years of her life spinning around a jagged triangle among the roles of rescuer, prosecutor, and victim. Right now, Derrick was playing the victim and asking her to play the rescuer.

Tomorrow, after she'd rescued him, she'd slide into prosecutor mode, and he'd stay right there as the victim. Only then he'd consider himself her victim, because she'd be angry.

And maybe none of that was on his mind right now. Maybe all he wanted was what all the men she'd known since she left home had wanted from her. It might be as simple as that. Well, that was an ugly, potholed road she'd traveled before. She knew exactly where it led.

But she saw something else in Derrick.

Something darker. Something... there was that word again. Desperate.

He said, "Please come back to bed."

"You need to go."

He let his arm drop to the mattress, turned his back to her, and stood. When he faced her again, his expression had shifted. His mouth was tight and angry, his eyes blazing. "You're serious? I can't stay?"

"You're not yourself. I don't know what happened or why, but if we ever do"—she waved toward the bed—"that, it'll be when you're acting like the man I met in Vegas. Not when you're behaving like this."

His eyes narrowed. "I had a difficult night. And you didn't help. You barely paid any attention to Constantine, even though I told you how important it was that I impress him."

"He's a blowhard who treats his girlfriend like dirt. I'm not about to suck up to a man like that. Apparently, that's your job."

"Yeah, it is my job." His whisper became vehement. "To ingratiate myself with wealthy people so they'll invest with me. That's what I do."

"Doesn't your work stand on its own?"

"Men like Constantine need to be respected."

"Brown-nosed, you mean. Why would you want to work with someone like that?"

"You have any idea what his account would be worth?"

"Money isn't everything. Not if it makes you behave like this."

His expression hardened into something she'd never seen on his features before. He moved toward her.

She took a step back and clenched her fists for the second time in ten minutes.

He froze. Blinked twice. His shoulders sagged, and he sat on the bed. "I'm sorry. You're right. I'm not myself."

She released her breath. After a moment, she sat beside him. "Go. Sleep. Things will be better tomorrow."

He said nothing as he stood and walked toward the door. He opened it, turned to face her, started to say something. Then, he clamped his lips shut, stepped out, and closed the door softly behind him.

Harper collapsed onto her pillow and thought about the man she'd just witnessed. If you examined anything long enough, you'd see all its facets. And its flaws.

CHAPTER THIRTEEN

The next morning, Harper slid the curtains back to discover clouds had moved in. She checked the weather on her cell. Apparently, the storm Derrick had assured her was supposed to move offshore had changed its course. So much for the day at the beach.

She dressed quickly in shorts and a T-shirt and tiptoed down the stairs. The house was quiet except for some gentle sounds coming from the kitchen. Maybe she could get in a walk on the sand before the rain started, but it would be rude to leave without at least saying good morning. She headed toward the voices and found Russell and Betts at the table enjoying a cup of coffee. Russell was reading the *Wall Street Journal*, and Betts had a Bible open in front of her. She looked up. "How'd you sleep?"

Of course Betts would be sweet, even before eight a.m. Harper figured she'd better not tell them about her middle-of-the-night visitor. "Very well, thanks."

Russell set the paper down and pushed back in his chair. "Can I get you some coffee?"

"No, thanks."

He settled again. "If you change your mind"—he pointed to the pot and the cups beside it—"help yourself."

"I thought I'd take a walk before the rain sets in."

Betts's gaze shifted to the wall of glass on the far side of the room. "It's not the weather we'd hoped for. You need anything before you go?"

"Nope. Just... should I go out the front?"

Russell said, "The porch door's unlocked."

She thanked them and left. The air was cooler than it had been the night before but thick with moisture and the scent of rain. She crossed the boardwalk and headed for the water. She hadn't bothered with shoes. Beaches were for bare feet. Once she hit the damp sand, she turned south. Despite the clouds, the morning was beautiful. The gunmetal-gray water, the slate-colored clouds. It wasn't idyllic, but it stirred her. Storms always did that. Reminded her of the thunderstorms that used to roll across the prairie when she was a little girl. She'd look out her window and gaze at the lightning, then count until the boom of thunder hit. She'd eagerly watch the news for reports of tornados, even after watching *The Wizard of Oz*. When she was a kid, Harper'd secretly wanted to be in a tornado, to experience what it would be like to have the wind lift her from her feet, to throw her off balance.

She hadn't been afraid of storms. No, she'd loved them. The interruption of normal life. The drama.

What a foolish child she'd been. Today, she knew what real storms were. She knew what it was like to have life lift you off your feet and smash you into the wall. She knew what it was like to look around and realize you had no idea how you got where you were, and you had no way out.

Oz had lost its allure.

The wind shifted. The hair on her arms stood, though not from a chill. She resisted the urge to look behind her, to study the dunes and peer between the shingled houses that lined the beach. Because, of course, nobody was watching her. Of course, she was safe here.

The energy of the storm—that's what had caused her nerves to fire like that, the hair to stand on end.

Even if she'd had a stalker back in Vegas, he wouldn't have followed her to the East Coast. Even if he'd wanted to, how would he have known where she was? Besides, there were plenty of women in Vegas. Why would anybody bother to trail her across the country?

She was safe.

The words became the beat she walked to as she continued down the shore. She repeated them until she almost believed them.

A drop of water plopped on her hand. She looked at it, then at the surf crashing just a few yards away. Ocean water, not rain. But a second plop landed on her bare shoulder. A third on her nose.

She turned back toward Russell and Betts's house. The more raindrops that landed, the faster she walked until she was running on the packed sand. The house came into view just as the deluge began. She sprinted the last fifty yards, but it was no use. By the time she reached the door to the screened-in porch, she was soaked.

Betts was waiting for her inside, a beach towel slung over her arm. "I was worried."

"A little rain never hurt anyone." She took the towel and dried off, shivering. "Wow, it got cold fast."

Russell stepped onto the porch beside his wife. "The water in the atmosphere is a lot colder than it is down here."

Suddenly, he reminded her of her father. The newspaper, the coffee, the weird facts added at just the right moment. She wanted to tell Russell that, tell him and Betts both how much she liked them, but it would sound silly and corny, so she settled for a huge smile. "I'll take that coffee now."

"I bet you will." His chuckle followed her as she headed inside.

"I'm just going to run upstairs and change, and I'll be right back."

Harper took a quick shower, brushed out her wet hair, and added a little makeup. By the time she returned to the kitchen, Russell had disappeared, and Kitty and Betts were at the table.

She headed toward the coffee and poured herself a cup. "What's going on?"

"We're cooking up a plan," Kitty said, "since the beach is out."

Harper added sugar and cream, then looked beyond the glass to the darkness that had settled outside. "What were you thinking?"

"The outlet mall!" Kitty seemed giddy at the prospect.

Harper tried to match her enthusiasm, but the thought of spending all day in and out of shops didn't appeal at all. Even if she had money to spend, which she didn't, she hated shopping.

Betts shook her head at her friend's glee, then focused on Harper. "Does that sound like fun, or do you have another idea?"

"Shopping is fine." She slipped into a chair at the table.

"We'll have a nice lunch out," Betts said, "my treat. That'll break up the day a little."

"Will the guys go with us?" Harper asked.

"Geez, I hope not," Kitty said. "Shopping with Keith is like dragging around a two-hundred-pound bag of sand all day long. Grouchy sand."

Harper giggled. "Derrick likes to shop, but if the rest of the guys aren't going, he probably won't either."

Betts said, "Considering how late they stayed up last night, I think most of them will sleep the day away."

"Did Russell stay up?" Harper asked. "Because he was awake early."

"Until about twelve-thirty. He'll wake up at six, no matter what time he goes to bed. We're alike in that way."

"You two are alike in a million ways," Kitty said. "Was it always like that, or did you grow more alike as the years went by?"

Betts seemed to consider the question. "I think... Hmm. We're alike in some ways. Our sleeping habits, for one thing. We both love to entertain. Neither of us likes to watch TV very much. We're both pretty high-energy. I guess we've grown more alike. But we didn't start that way. Our relationship was built on some pretty sandy soil when we first got married."

Harper leaned forward. "That's hard to believe, seeing you now. What changed?"

Betts shrugged, smiled. "We met Jesus."

"Oh." Harper hadn't expected that.

Kitty sighed. "Now you've done it." But her words were amused. "You've opened the door, and Betts never ceases to go through that particular door."

Betts just laughed. "She asked."

"I did." Harper kept her focus on Betts. "We went to church when I was a kid. It didn't seem to make much difference in our lives. I've been going lately with the man I take care of."

"Going to church and walking with Jesus are two very different things," Betts said. "Nothing against church, of course. We go faithfully when we're home. But going to church for a lot of people is about looking good on the outside. Walking with Jesus is about getting good from the inside out. It's about giving God access to your whole heart."

Her whole heart? Why would God want that? The thought of Him seeing everything in her heart made her shudder. But Betts seemed so peaceful. "And that helped your marriage?"

Betts's nod was emphatic. "As we both sought to be closer to God, we couldn't help but get closer to each other."

"Seems simplistic," Kitty said. "No offense."

"Like a lot of things in life," Betts said, "walking with God is simple, but it's not easy." She sipped her coffee and stood. "You ladies want some breakfast?"

"Not if we're going out to lunch," Kitty said. "Because I know you'll serve a yummy dinner at the party."

"Mostly appetizers tonight," Betts said. "I'm having the party catered so I won't have to cook all day."

Harper's stomach growled at the mention of breakfast. "I don't want you to have to cook for me. Maybe just some toast?"

A few minutes later while Betts and Kitty planned their shopping excursion, Harper nibbled her toast and thought about what Betts had said.

Good from the inside out.

Red's words had been different, but the sentiment was similar to what he'd been telling her. That Jesus could forgive her sins. He *wanted* to forgive her. He *wanted* to wash her ugliness away.

Could it be true? Could Harper really be free of her past?

Russell came into the kitchen and kissed his wife on the cheek before settling into a chair. They shared a smile. Then, he picked up the newspaper, and Betts went back to her conversation.

The love between the two of them, the love that seemed to glow all around them, couldn't be denied. Did God have something to do with that?

Was God the key? With Him, would it really be possible for Harper to know that sort of love?

CHAPTER FOURTEEN

Shopping was more fun than she'd thought it would be, thanks to the company. Kitty not only oohed and aahed over everything, but she cracked jokes and kept them laughing from the moment they left the house. Jenny had joined them. She'd barely spoken in the morning, but as the day went on, she came out of her shell. Turned out, she had a flair for fashion, and she and Marjorie bonded over that. Harper'd planned to just browse, but Jenny convinced her to try on clothes. In one store, she and Marjorie dressed her up and accessorized her like a mannequin. They had a great time doing it. Harper pretended to enjoy it until she found she actually did.

She hadn't had real female friends since high school. She'd forgotten how fun they could be.

When they got back to the house that afternoon, the guys were sitting on the porch watching the rain outside, already sipping from bottles of beer.

"Constantine's holding court again." Marjorie dropped her purchases on the floor by the stairs.

The woman had done a complete turnabout in her opinion of Constantine. Harper followed her gaze and looked again. Sure enough, Keith, Carter, and Derrick were nodding as Constantine spoke.

Russell was staring at the surf, sipping from a glass of what looked like water.

"Constantine's got charisma." Betts filled the coffee carafe with water. "Always has."

Jenny's *pfft* had them all looking at her.

She realized all eyes were on her and reddened. "What?" When nobody spoke, she said, "He can be charming. When people are watching."

Betts set the carafe in the coffee maker and focused on Jenny. "And when people aren't watching?"

Jenny shrugged. "It's nothing."

But it wasn't nothing. After they filled their coffee cups, Harper pulled out a kitchen chair and nodded to it. Jenny slid in, and Harper sat beside her and rested her hand over Jenny's. "Does he ever hurt you?"

"No. Not like that. Just... He can be cruel."

Betts took the chair on Jenny's other side. "Charming, charismatic, but when Constantine doesn't get what he wants, he's mean. He was like that in college. I never kowtowed to him, and he didn't like it. He made some cruel remarks about me. Some cutting remarks *to* me. Honestly, I didn't think his friendship with Russell would survive it."

"It did, though," Kitty said. "How come? Russell doesn't seem like the type of guy who'd put up with that."

"He didn't. He told Constantine to knock it off or they were through. Impervious though he seems, Connie needs Russell. Russell keeps him grounded. Years ago, after Connie made his first few millions, he came to our house all braggadocios. Russell wasn't impressed and told him so. And Connie... I think he needed to hear it. I think that's why he came."

Jenny's gaze hadn't wavered from Betts's face. "That's my problem. That's why he doesn't take me seriously or treat me with respect. I always... how'd you put it? I kowtow to him. I cower. I never stand up for myself. I never argue with him. I never call him out when he lies to me or treats me badly. I just put up with it."

Harper could relate. She'd allowed herself to be treated like property. Like decoration. Shame inched its way into her heart, but she forced it out. She wasn't that woman anymore.

She never would be again.

"And as long as you put up with it," Betts said, "he'll continue to treat you like he does."

The doorbell rang, and Betts left to answer it. A moment later, women in chef's coats carried platters and trays into the kitchen. Betts followed. "You girls might want to go into the living room. It's about to get busy in here."

Kitty and Marjorie headed upstairs to get ready for the party. Betts stayed in the kitchen with the caterers. Harper sat on the comfy brown sofa and gestured for Jenny to join her.

Jenny settled in and set her coffee on the table, then turned to Harper. "I know what you're saying, you and Betts. And I know you're right. But what if I stand up to him and he dumps me?"

"No man is worth losing yourself over."

"You say that as if you're sure."

"It's a lesson I paid a really steep price for." Steep didn't begin to cover it. The things she'd done, the way she'd sold her soul for some counterfeit version of love. She'd trusted men, and one by one, they'd all let her down. The only exceptions were bald or gray-headed, too old to do any damage. And even them she had a hard time trusting. "I'll never allow myself to be used by a man again. Never."

Jenny sat back and swallowed. She reached for her coffee cup and took a long sip. Her hand was shaking.

Harper squeezed her hand and pushed her own demons aside. She needed Jenny to understand all of it. "It's very likely he'll dump you at some point. I wish I could tell you differently, but what I see in your relationship isn't love. It's power on his part, submission on yours. I can't see how he's going to take you seriously at this point, no matter what you do. You have to decide if you'd rather live like this or live without him."

"I was destitute before I met him. Now..." But her words trailed off.

"Now, you have a lot of nice stuff. Beautiful clothes, lovely jewelry. But life isn't about stuff."

Jenny swallowed, looked at the blank TV screen, and said nothing.

Harper looked beyond Jenny to the men on the porch. Constantine's gaze locked with hers. He narrowed his eyes. She broke the eye contact.

The hair on her arms stood again, and it wasn't from the cold.

CHAPTER FIFTEEN

That night, people kept coming until the beach house looked like it might burst at the seams. Of course, when Betts and Russell had invited all their friends for the party, they'd thought the weather would be nice. Harper imagined how different it would be if guests could gather on the patio and on the beach. That kind of party would be lovely. But this... She surveyed the huge crowd. There were well-dressed people sitting on every chair and standing on nearly every square foot of floor space. Harper stood a few steps up on the staircase and tried to talk herself into continuing down. She'd already been in that mess, had been introduced to so many people that all their faces were blending together. Perfectly coiffed blondes and brunettes dripping with jewelry, dignified gentlemen with open collars and sports coats, all holding drinks and nibbling appetizers and talking about people Harper didn't know and businesses Harper didn't understand.

Who could have blamed her for escaping to her bedroom for a few minutes of privacy? She wondered, had she stayed up there, if anybody would have noticed her absence. Not that she minded. Aside from Jenny, whom she hadn't seen, Harper's new friends were having fun. They knew the people here tonight. They enjoyed this kind of thing. Harper would rather be home with Red.

Near the front door, Jenny and Constantine were engaged in a private discussion. It was the first time Harper'd seen the man not surrounded by sycophants, though plenty seemed to be hovering nearby. That morning, before they'd left for shopping, she and Derrick had found a few moments alone on the porch, and she'd asked him about Constantine, trying to understand why the man was so well respected.

Derrick had rolled his eyes. "You're the only person here who doesn't know the answer to that question. He's worth hundreds of millions of dollars."

Hundreds of millions? No wonder people hung on his every word. Apparently, he'd invested in offshore oil and drilling technology. Not to mention real estate.

Apparently, being rich recommended a person to this crowd. She didn't belong here.

Jenny didn't fit in, either. The woman dressed the part, but she certainly didn't act it. It seemed she and Constantine were embroiled in a battle. By her feet... was that a suitcase?

Indeed it was. A moment later, Jenny snatched it and walked out.

Good for her.

Harper wanted to shout her support. All her boredom whooshed away with the closing of that door.

Jenny'd done it. And maybe, just maybe, Harper had given her a little encouragement.

All the junk she'd gone through, maybe sharing it had made a difference. Maybe all those years and experiences hadn't been a complete waste.

Constantine stared at the closed door a moment, then turned, a plastic smile on his face. Not ten seconds went by before people surrounded him. She couldn't hear them, of course, but she could imagine the flattering and fawning. He responded, but then he saw Harper on the stairs. Their gazes met.

She turned away, noticed Derrick and Keith on the porch. Harper started to head their way, then paused and looked closer.

They were arguing, too. Derrick was red-faced. Keith jabbed his finger in Derrick's chest. What was going on?

It couldn't be good. And Keith was a cop. Was Derrick in some sort of legal trouble?

If he was, Harper needed to know immediately. She'd had her fill of people living on the edge of the law. What else could it be?

Derrick slammed out the screen door and into the night.

What in the world? She hadn't gotten the feeling he and Keith had known each other that well. And now... there was definitely something there, something Harper knew nothing about.

When Keith turned back toward the party, Harper thought about following Derrick. Except that by the time she shouldered her way through the crowd and to the door, he'd probably be long gone. And he seemed angry. Maybe now wasn't the best time to talk. She'd ask him about it later.

Harper tried to find someone to talk to and watched Kitty as she snatched a blanket off the back of the couch, wrapped it around her shoulders, and joined her husband on the porch. A moment later, they, too, were involved in a serious discussion.

What was that about? Did it have something to do with Derrick?

Why was Harper the only one who didn't know?

Harper was just about to escape back up the stairs when she heard someone behind her. She turned and saw Betts heading down.

"You all right?"

"Just trying to work up my courage."

Betts laughed. "Come on. I'll introduce you around."

It was the last thing Harper wanted to do, but she followed anyway, met Betts's friends, and made small talk. Usually, when people realized who she was (nobody important) and what she did (nothing impressive), they nodded politely and looked for the bigger, better deal. Betts wouldn't realize that, of course. She saw the best in everyone. Saw it when it wasn't even there to see.

Not thirty minutes had passed when Harper found herself alone, again, in a sea of bodies. She leaned against the living room wall, sipped a glass of tea that needed more sugar, and watched, wishing like crazy she'd escaped when she had the chance.

A moment later, she felt a presence beside her and turned. Constantine.

He was no taller than she was, though his presence seemed to loom large over the room. She hadn't been this close to him all weekend, and she didn't like it. Didn't like the strength he emanated, the confidence. The anger. She looked around for his ever-present posse, but he was alone.

He stared out at partygoers. "Having fun?"

She followed his gaze, happy not to have to look into his eyes. There was something...menacing there. "Sure."

"You're lying. You hate it."

She glanced at him, forced a smile. "Okay, I hate it. You seem to be enjoying yourself."

He shrugged. "You know what I don't enjoy?" He paused, seemed to wait for her to answer. She couldn't imagine and couldn't care less. He leaned closer and whispered, "Sleeping alone."

Acid pooled in her stomach. She didn't react to his words. She'd known men like this one. Like dogs, they could smell fear. "Sorry to hear that."

"Good to know, considering it's your fault."

She turned to face him then, tamping down the fear in favor of the irritation that rose. "How do you figure?"

"Jenny left."

Harper turned toward the crowd so he wouldn't see her satisfied smile. "Good for her."

Constantine's hand slithered around Harper's wrist. Soft and smooth, strong as cushioned handcuffs.

She considered trying to yank her arm back, but she knew it would do no good. Better to pretend she didn't care.

"Not so good for me," he said.

"That's not my problem."

He shifted closer. "It's your opportunity." Instinct had her yanking at her hand, but he tightened his grip. "Your boyfriend needs me. He needs my money. Tonight, you can make all his troubles go away."

How dare he? Did she look like a prostitute? Or did he think everyone was for sale if you had enough money. She clenched her hands into fists and contemplated a good, loud scream.

People would probably accuse her of harming their hero.

And then, the rest of his words registered.

Derrick's troubles? What did Constantine know that she didn't?

That he had troubles that money would solve, obviously.

She pushed that thought away. First, she had to deal with this... this... She couldn't even come up with a bad enough word.

She forced herself to think. She didn't want to make a scene. She wanted this man away from her. Now. She took a calming breath and blew it out. Then she faced him full on. "So you're saying that if we spend this one night together, you'll move your investment accounts to Derrick?"

"Some of them."

"For how long?"

A slow smile spread across his lips. "I guess that depends on how much fun we have."

She forced a laugh, leaned very close. Waited until he'd become quite sure of her. The slithering snake. "I've done a whole list of bad things in my life, *Connie*."

He flinched at the name.

"Things I'm not proud of. But I've never been a whore, and I'm not about to add that to the list tonight."

His smile faded. "Not a whore. An opportunist."

"So here's the deal," she said. "You're going to release my wrist or I'm going to scream and embarrass us both. And if you set one foot near my bedroom tonight, you'll regret it."

"Like you could stop me."

"You want to risk it?" After a little shrug, she added, "I spent a couple of years in prison."

His eyes widened, and his jaw dropped.

"I learned a few tricks there." She glanced toward the kitchen doorway. "Have you seen Betts's knife collection?"

He released her arm and stepped back.

She smiled at the doubt in his expression. The wavering confidence in his eyes. "You have fun now, Connie."

CHAPTER SIXTEEN

Back in her bedroom, Harper changed out of her party clothes and scrubbed her face. Before she climbed into bed, she perched her ratty old suitcase against the door. If anybody opened it, the thing would topple over.

At least she'd have a moment's notice before anybody got in. If she'd brought her keys, she'd have pulled out the little keychain/knife Estelle had given her. Like a fool, she'd left her keys on the bureau in her bedroom at Red's.

She couldn't get back home fast enough. The sooner she put this night behind her, the happier she'd be.

Not that she'd be able to sleep after Constantine's proposition. The disgusting creep.

She was reading while the party raged downstairs when she heard a soft knock on her door.

"Who is it?"

Derrick called, "You came upstairs without saying good-night."

She'd seen him once after the incident with Constantine. He'd been across the room, dripping rainwater and talking to someone she hadn't met. He'd laughed as if his walk in the rain had been a lark.

He hadn't noticed her, and she hadn't gone to him.

Now, she crossed the room and moved the suitcase to open the door. He stood on the other side in his green shirt and khakis. At least they were dry. He looked... defeated. "You all right?"

He stepped past her and sat on the end of her bed. He was silent a moment too long. When he spoke, his words were measured. "I just need to ask you..."

When his voice trailed off, she cocked her head to the side. "What?"

"Did you think of me at all when you told Jenny she should leave?"

"Oh." She hadn't. She didn't realize Derrick knew anything about that. She closed the bedroom door and stood in front of him. "What did Constantine tell you?"

Derrick swallowed, and his lips flattened. He took a deep breath. "He said you talked Jenny into leaving him, and she did. He was laughing when he said it, like it was all so funny, so we all laughed with him. But I could tell by the way he looked at me... He didn't think it was funny. And he blames you."

"It's not my fault he treats his girlfriend like dirt."

"So you did tell her—?"

"I suggested that he'd never respect her if she didn't respect herself."

Derrick smoothed the bedspread, nodded slowly.

She thought about telling him about Constantine's proposition. Maybe he'd be angry. Maybe he'd be indignant that the man would dare. But she feared there'd be a little spark of something else in his response. Hope, maybe. As if he wouldn't mind trading her for a solution to all his troubles.

She kept her conversation with Constantine to herself. Her opinion of Derrick had fallen enough this weekend. The wrong reaction from him would make that opinion plummet beyond repair. Besides, she had something more pressing to say.

"What were you and Keith arguing about?"

He blinked, looked up, then back at the blankets. "Nothing, really. Nothing important."

"Looked important from where I stood."

He met her gaze with narrowed eyes. "Where was that? Were you listening?"

"I was on the stairs. I saw you guys through the windows. Why? Was it something you wouldn't want me to hear?"

"I'm managing it."

"Managing what? Are you involved in something illegal? Because if you are—"

"It's nothing like that."

"I can't be involved with you if you're doing something illegal. No way."

"It's nothing to worry about." He reached forward, took her hands, and looked up at her. "I promise. It's nothing to worry about."

"But he's a detective. What else—?"

"He does some work for a guy on the side."

"What kind of work?"

Derrick sighed, took off his glasses, and rubbed his eyes. "It's a long story."

"I have nowhere to go."

He slid the glasses back on. "I owe some money to this guy, and Keith works for him."

"You owe money... like, to a banker?"

"Not exactly."

And then she got it. She jerked her hands free, paced toward the bathroom, and turned. "A bookie?"

"No. Sort of." The slump of his shoulders told her much more than his words could. "I didn't want you to find out. I'm trying to fix it."

"How much?"

He shrugged. "A lot."

"Are we talking hundreds or thousands?"

He stood and stepped toward her. "It's not your problem, Harper."

The pieces were falling into place. All the trips to Vegas. This summer, Red had gotten sick, and she'd called Derrick and told him not to come up for the weekend. He'd gone to Atlantic City instead.

He'd been back a number of times. He said he had clients there he had to visit. But maybe he'd only gone to gamble. And then there was the poker game the night before.

The truth held her in place like lead shoes. "You're addicted."

"Not addicted. Not like that." He ran his fingers through his hair. "I can fix it. You have no idea how good I am at poker. I'm the luckiest guy you've ever met." He offered his charming smile. "Obviously I'm lucky. I won you, didn't I?"

She wasn't stupid enough to fall for that. She crossed her arms and waited.

He sighed. "I'm working on it."

Right. He had it under control. He could get a handle on it. It wasn't a problem.

She'd been there before. She'd seen addiction. She wasn't going back to that circus. No way. "That's what this weekend was about, trying to get more business so you can pay off your gambling debts."

His mouth closed, tightened. He said nothing

She crossed the room and pulled back the curtains to stare at the darkness outside. To think. Waves smashed against the sand as if they had a grudge. The murmur of voices and laughter from the party filtered up through the floor and added to the loneliness infecting her like a virus. Because Derrick was with her. But his heart didn't belong to her.

It belonged to gambling.

How pathetic, for both of them.

At least now she knew Derrick's *troubles*. The reason he'd seemed desperate all weekend was because he was desperate.

Constantine knew about it. Keith knew. Who else? Did everybody know but Harper? Had they all been feeling *sorry* for her? Because she had such lousy taste in men. She'd been so proud, trying to help Jenny, when she should have been taking her own advice. They probably thought Harper was a fool. Why did she always do this, let herself believe?

At least she hadn't slept with him.

She let the curtain fall and turned. "How much?"

"I'm going to have to ask Gramps for the money. I was trying to avoid it, but I don't see that I have any choice now."

"How much?"

"A lot, okay?" His voice rose in volume and pitch—anger and embarrassment. "A lot."

"And then last night... Was that a friendly game of poker, like you said? Or was it high-stakes?"

He met her eyes. "It started friendly." And then his gaze slid away.

"And you went deeper into debt."

He said nothing, just stared at the floor.

"Do you owe money to anyone downstairs?"

"I paid Carter off. I had a little in my account."

She sat on the side of the bed. She felt sorry for him, she did. Except that he'd lied to her all along.

He circled the bed and sat beside her. His arm slid around her back.

She had to force herself not to pull away.

He hung his head. "I'll get help. I'll start going to those stupid meetings. Maybe do the twelve-step program."

She nodded, stared at the gauzy curtains, imagined the beach outside. If only she could sail away, avoid all of this.

He turned to her, and she forced herself to return the gaze. Everything about his expression said *trust me*. Round face, warm brown eyes, nerdy glasses. He dressed impeccably and had a good job. He'd been kind, treated her with respect. But he couldn't be trusted.

"I'm going to fix this," he said. "I've gotten myself into a mess before, and I've always managed to get myself out. But without you... Please, don't leave me." He took her hands and squeezed. "I need you, Harper."

"I can't be involved in anything illegal."

"You're not. You won't be. I'll get myself together. You and me, we'll be strong together. Promise me you won't let this come between us."

"You've let it come between us. All weekend, it's come between us. For weeks, it's come between us."

He nodded along with her words. "You're right. I didn't know how to tell you, but now I have. Now, we can be a team. You can help me with this, the way I helped you with the job for Gramps."

Wait, what? What was he suggesting, some sort of quid pro quo?

Her feelings must've shown on her face, because he said, "Not like that. Not like you owe me. I'm just saying, I trusted, despite your past, because I knew you. I know you. And you know me. You know I'd never hurt you. You know I care for you. Yes, I have a problem, and I need to fix it. But I'm more than just a gambler." He released her hands and brushed her hair away from her face. "I'm a good guy, Harper. You know this about me."

"I know. You are."

He leaned closer. "I have a good job, a solid future."

She smiled. "I don't care about that."

"I know. That's one of the reasons I love you."

"Oh." He'd never said that to her before. He'd told her he needed her. She knew he wanted her. But love?

"You don't have to say it back." He rested his palm against her cheek. "You're not ready. It's okay. But just know, despite all the stupid stuff I've done this weekend, I love you. My love for you is the best thing about me."

Love? Was that what this was? Wasn't love supposed to be honest, selfless?

"You're not there yet." He traced her hairline with the tip of his finger. "It's okay. I'm willing to wait for you as long as it takes."

He leaned in and kissed her, slowly at first, then with a passion she couldn't resist. He lowered her to the bed, never releasing her from the kiss.

It would have been so easy to let it happen. He loved her. He'd said so. And look at all he'd done for her.

But he had a problem, a serious problem.

And she wouldn't be a fool again.

She pushed him away. "No. I'm not—"

"Please. Please don't send me away."

"I can't do this."

"You can. It'll be different with me." His hands roved and roamed, and she squirmed, tried to keep them in safe places. "Come on. You can trust me."

Could she? He'd kept his addiction from her. He'd kept the truth about his debt from her. Which proved she couldn't trust him.

"No."

He dropped his face to her shoulder. "Please. Don't send me away."

"Go to bed, Derrick."

He stood and stared down at her. "To bed?" He raked his fingers through his hair. "You think I can sleep now?"

"I'm sorry. I just—"

"Whatever." He yanked the door open, stepped into the hall, and slammed it behind him.

She listened to his footfalls until they faded. Then, she crossed the room and leaned her suitcase against the door again. To heck with Derrick. With Constantine. With Carter. If the suitcase fell, she'd scream her head off.

CHAPTER SEVENTEEN

arper woke to sun streaming in through the curtains. She pulled them back and gazed out at the morning. Amazing what a difference a few hours could make. The blue of the sky was broken up by a few big, puffy clouds. There were already families and joggers on the beach. Although the weather was lovely, waves still pummeled the shore.

She dressed in a T-shirt and shorts and slipped out the patio door before anybody saw her. Even though the weather was tranquil and the people cheerful, she couldn't settle her thoughts. She wanted to regret coming on this trip, but she couldn't quite get there. She was glad to have met Russell and Betts. Their marriage was so filled with peace. Like Red, they were content. But what was special about them was that they were happy together. At peace together.

Could she ever find that with a man?

The question was so foolish, she scoffed. She'd come on this trip to find out what Derrick was hiding. Well, now she knew.

Every man she'd ever trusted had let her down. Her first serious boyfriend had hired her for his show in Vegas and had fired her when she'd broken up with him. Her second boyfriend had landed her in prison. Derrick had kept his gambling addiction from her. Then there were all the other men she'd met along the way, the drunk, drooling, disgusting men who frequented the club where she had worked. Men like Constantine, who treated her like a shiny toy in a storefront, available for purchase for the right price.

She wanted the sea breeze to carry the next thought away, but there it was. Even her father had failed her. He'd raised her in the church, taught her right from wrong. He'd thrown around words like *love* and *grace* and *mercy* all her life. But when she'd chosen wrong and ended up in prison, he'd rejected her. *Don't call here again.*

Men like Russell, men like Red... They might be out there, but they were taken or too old. Definitely too scarce. She'd never met a man like that who was her age, available, and attracted to her, and based on her track record—and her baggage—she never would.

Which left her with men like Derrick.

It wasn't his addiction that bothered her. Yes, that was an issue. Living in Vegas, she'd seen the effects of a gambling addiction. Formerly successful people reduced to poverty and, often, homelessness. People whose blind hope that the next game would be the game that saved them from all their troubles. She'd seen panhandlers take their meager funds into casinos, certain this would be the day for their big score.

She'd also known and heard of plenty of people who'd overcome the addiction. If Derrick were willing, he could overcome it, too. But the fact that he'd lied about it said a lot about where he stood. So did the fact that he thought Harper could rescue him.

She knew better than to think she could pull him from the deep water. She was barely surviving herself. Derrick might just take them both down.

She was nearing the house, hoping Derrick was awake so they could head back to Red's, when she heard people on the porch. With the bright sun beating down on her, she could barely make out who was there. When she heard Derrick's voice, she paused.

"Look." The pitch was too high, too eager. "I know it looked bad this weekend. I've just hit a rough patch. But that doesn't affect—"

"I'm sorry." Russell, so calm and steady. "Not forever. Just until you grow up a little, settle into your success."

Harper stepped around the corner of the house and out of their line of sight. She shouldn't eavesdrop. On the other hand, maybe this was her only opportunity to find out what was really going on.

Derrick said, "I'd never gamble with your money."

"I believe that," Russell said, "but when people dig themselves into holes, they do things they wouldn't otherwise do. And from what I overheard last night, you're in deep."

Overheard? Had he heard the conversation between Derrick and her? No, probably not. So maybe he'd overheard the conversation between Derrick and Keith on the porch. Maybe he knew more than Harper did.

"None of that affects the kind of stockbroker I am. I'm good at what I do."

"One of the best I've ever worked with," Russell said. "But when I give someone access to my money, I need to know I can trust them. Unfortunately, after your behavior last night, I don't trust you anymore."

"It was just one game!"

A cloud drifted in front of the sun. Harper peeked around the corner and saw inside the screened-in porch. Derrick was seated on one of the chairs, his head rolled forward. Russell stood beside him, his hand on Derrick's shoulder.

"Here's the thing," Russell said. "This is not the end for you. You need to get yourself together, keep working hard, and quit gambling. Go to Gamblers Anonymous and seek that higher power they talk about. In fact, do more than that. Seek God, the only real God. He can help you overcome this. If you ever have any questions about God, don't hesitate to call me."

Derrick might have said something, but she didn't hear it.

Russell walked into the house and closed the slider behind him.

At that moment, Derrick looked up. His gaze locked with hers.

She took a few steps toward him but froze at the expression on his face. Despair mixed with pure fury.

After a deep breath, she stepped inside the porch and sat beside him.

"I guess you heard everything?"

"Just the end."

"Not only did I not get Constantine as a client, I lost Russell's business."

"I'm sorry."

He nodded slowly, staring beyond her. "I guess none of it matters to you."

"What's that supposed to mean?"

"You cost me my shot with Constantine."

She sighed. "I didn't mean to hurt you. It never crossed my mind that Jenny would tell him I'd told her to leave. I didn't. I just told her to stand up for herself."

"Whether you meant it or not..." His voice trailed off. "And then last night, after you kicked me out, I went back downstairs."

"And played poker," she guessed.

He said nothing, which was as much of an admission as anything.

"And lost big," she said.

He shrugged.

"And you blame me."

His gaze snapped to hers. "If you'd let me stay—"

"You don't get to blame me for your bad choices, Derrick. You could have gone to bed. You should have."

"I was too keyed up."

"You could have gone for a walk. You could've read a book. You could've gone back downstairs and not gambled. You could've done a lot of things besides play poker."

"I know that." He raked his hands through his hair. "Don't you think I've gone over all the things I could have done differently? Don't you think I regret it enough? Thanks for piling on."

She didn't like this Derrick one bit. She liked the sweet, generous man she'd met in Vegas. She liked the confident man who'd shown up at the house on Friday. She didn't like this accusing, angry man. She didn't like him, and she didn't think she'd ever trust him again.

CHAPTER EIGHTEEN

The only thing good about the long drive home was the lack of traffic. The tension in the car was palpable but dwarfed by that at the house when they'd left.

Harper had hugged and thanked Russell and Betts, who were kind and gracious, as always. Kitty was extra nice to her, inviting her to send along her resume if Harper decided to change jobs. She thanked her for the kindness but knew she never would. No chance any doctor or hospital would hire a nurse with a felony on her record. Keith was quiet, as usual, but grasped her hand and muttered, "It was nice to meet you."

Fortunately, Marjorie, Carter, and Constantine had still been upstairs when she and Derrick left, keeping the good-byes to a minimum.

As kind as the two couples were to them, tension hung over the group like the stench of bad fish as Derrick shook the men's hands and kissed the women's cheeks. Did everybody know about his conversation with Russell? About the poker game?

Only when they pulled into the circle drive in front of Red's house did Harper let herself begin to relax. She couldn't wait to get inside and away from Derrick. He put the car in park, and she reached for the door handle. He stopped her with a hand on her forearm. "Can we talk for a sec?"

"We've been in the car together for hours, and now you want to talk?"

"I'm sorry. I'm just... I don't know what to say."

She stepped out of the car. Derrick climbed out on the far side and popped the trunk. He snatched her suitcase, slid out the handle, but didn't let it go. "Five minutes."

"Okay."

He took a deep breath and looked at the house behind her a moment. "I'm sorry."

"I bet you are."

"Not for..." He hung his head. "Of all the stupid stuff I did this weekend, I'm most sorry about how I treated you."

She considered minimizing it, letting him off the hook. But she kept her mouth shut.

"I didn't pay enough attention to you," he said. "I knew Carter was hitting on you, but I was focused on Russell and Constantine, and I figured you could handle yourself."

"I can."

"I know, but you shouldn't have had to. I should have been there for you."

He was right. He should have. She acknowledged that with a nod.

"And I'm sorry for not telling you about the gambling. I just thought, when I met you... When I'm with you, I don't think of gambling. I thought I was over it. All those times I came to see you in Vegas, I didn't gamble once."

"Really?"

"I didn't think I needed to tell you because I thought it was managed."

"What happened?"

"You were home with Gramps when he was sick, and I thought, just one night in Atlantic City... I thought it would be fine. But I got in over my head. Then, I kept going back, trying to fix it."

"Just making it worse," she guessed.

"I already owed this guy money, and now I'm in really deep."

"How deep?"

He blew out a long breath. "Couple hundred thousand."

"Whoa." She stepped back, caught her breath. "Are you kidding me?"

"I know, I know." He raked his fingers through his hair. "I've really messed up. The guy I owe is really pressing me for the money."

"So what are you going to do?"

He shrugged. "I'll figure it out." He stepped toward her and smiled. "It's not your problem, Harper. I know I should have told you, and I hope you can forgive me for that. I hope... I know you're probably plotting your escape as we speak." He smiled when he said the words, but she saw the flicker of worry in his eyes. "I just want to ask you... and I have no right to ask you for anything. I know that. But can you please give me some time to make all this right?" He stepped forward, so close she could feel his breath on her cheeks. "Don't give up on me yet, Harper. I need you."

She hadn't made up her mind about him, and while his apology helped, there was no guarantee he'd be able to do everything he'd promised. Her instinct was to break up with him. To distance herself. With her only serious boyfriends in the past, she'd told herself that she should have gotten out sooner. Depended on herself. If she cut bait now, she could save herself a lot of grief.

Frankly, she'd probably end things with Derrick. She should feel... what? Sad, depressed, let down? But she didn't. She cared about Derrick. She'd appreciated his kindness, his gifts, his concern when she lived in Vegas. But she'd fallen more for the idea of him—a successful man without all the baggage her previous boyfriends had hauled into the relationships.

She'd been wrong about that. Derrick had just hidden his baggage better.

Unless something monumental changed, she'd end things with him, but not today. Today, he'd been hurt enough. She'd hang in there a little longer. Maybe he'd surprise her, do everything he promised, and turn out to be her Prince Charming.

"Okay." She smiled at him and stepped back. "But from now on, you need to be honest with me."

He nodded, his eyes lighting up as if she'd just repaired his favorite toy. "Thank you."

"Are you going to hang around for a while?"

"I don't think so. I have some stuff I need to take care of before work tomorrow." Derrick carried her suitcase to the door and kissed her on the cheek.

As he walked back to his car, Harper had the feeling that more time wouldn't reveal Derrick as Prince Charming. Instead, she might only get a close-up glimpse of a frog.

CHAPTER NINETEEN

Harper carried her small bag upstairs to her bedroom, dropped it on the bed, and hurried back down in search of Red.

She found him in the wide backyard, standing in front of a rose bush, deadheading flowers.

She hurried out to meet him. "What are you doing?"

"Those gardeners don't know how to take care of Bebe's flowers." He snipped off an old bloom, dropped it in a plastic bag dangling from his wrist, and reached for another.

"What if you'd fallen?" Harper could imagine him struggling to stand back up on the uneven lawn.

He looked up, holding onto his fedora so it wouldn't fall, and surveyed the sky. "Sunny day. I'd have gotten a nice tan." He chuckled and continued with the roses.

"You're a stubborn old man, you know that?"

"I'm not old." He winked. "How was the beach? You got a whopper of a storm yesterday. I thought you might stay later today to soak up the sunshine."

"We were ready to get back."

Red dropped another spent rose in the plastic bag and peered at her with those sharp blue eyes. "Something happen?"

"No."

His lips closed while he studied her. "My grandson treat you well?"

She didn't want to lie to him but wasn't prepared to tell him the truth. "He spent a lot of time trying to drum up new accounts."

"Hmph." He inched around the bush.

She resisted the urge to suggest Red let the gardeners do it, or worse, assist him herself. He was in one of his I-don't-need-your-help moods, and offering would only irritate him.

Red cut another bloom and dropped it in the bag. "I love that boy, but sometimes I don't like him very much."

She'd gotten that impression before, but she'd never heard him say it. "Why is that?"

"He makes all the money he needs and more, but he spends it as fast as it comes in. Never has an extra dime."

"Maybe he'll learn to be wiser with it."

Another "hmph" told her what Red thought of that.

"His dad never did," Red said. "Died in serious debt. Mortgaged to the hilt. Used to gamble, that one." The words were delivered casually, but Red peered at her from beneath the rim of his hat and held her gaze.

"Oh... Well." It wasn't her place to tell Red about Derrick's gambling. She wasn't going to lie to the man, either. "That must have been hard for you."

"I like a risk." He turned his gaze back to the bright red blooms and continued snipping. "But I risked wisely. Risked in real estate. Only made safe bets. You buy a house, it's going to be worth something. It has intrinsic value. You work hard, keep it in good shape, do your best to keep renters in it while you make the payments, and the house goes up in value. If the market turns"—he shrugged—"you did your part. Maybe you lose a little here and there. But you don't lose everything. Gambling, though... That's not earning. That's trying to get something for nothing, and it never works."

She'd learned that lesson the hard way. She'd been sent to prison because her boyfriend and his friend had tried to take the easy way out, and they'd used her to help. She'd been ignorant of their schemes, but the judge hadn't believed her claim of innocence. All because Emmitt and Barry were too lazy to work and had already spent all the money she'd earned.

The memories didn't sit well. The comparison between Emmitt and Derrick turned in her stomach like a Tilt-A-Whirl.

"What happened to your son?"

Red maneuvered another foot around the bush until he was practically against the fence. "He and his wife were killed in a car accident. On their way home from Atlantic City. George had had too much to drink and swerved to miss a deer. Ended up driving into a tree."

"I'm so sorry."

"Long time ago." Red focused on the roses. "Derrick never told you?"

"Just that they passed away when he was eighteen. But he never told me how, and I never asked."

"Hard time for both of us." He pointed to a fading bloom out of his reach. "Get that one for me, would you?"

She took the pruners and cut off the bloom, then got a couple more she didn't think he could see from where he stood. While she worked, she thought of Derrick. She couldn't imagine the pain of burying both his parents at such a young age. Legally an adult, but not really. An age when he'd needed his father and mother. At least he'd had Red, who'd taken him in, sent him to college, and supported him all those years.

She handed Red the pruners.

"You don't have to stay out here with me, girl. I got this."

"I'm staying. Not because you need me"—not that he'd admit, anyway—"but because I missed you."

She had missed Red. He was kind and gentle and honest. And today he seemed as healthy as she'd ever seen him. His face was pink from the heat, but not frighteningly so. Another hour and he'd need to go inside, get out of the sun. But this morning, she figured the vitamin D was doing him good. His legs seemed strong. His smile was bright as he accomplished his task.

He probably didn't need her at all. But she stayed anyway, just in case. And because his peace, his kindness, were a balm to her raw nerves.

If she had any hope Derrick would turn out to be like Red, she'd stick it out with him through all the stuff—the gambling addiction, the debt. But Derrick wasn't like his grandfather. He was like his father. And look what a mess that man had left behind.

CHAPTER TWENTY

Derrick arrived for their date on Friday night bearing his suitcase and a handful of purple irises.

Harper glanced at the suitcase and took the bouquet. "You shouldn't have."

He kissed her on the cheek. "You deserve these and a million more."

She eyed the suitcase. "You're staying?"

"I thought I'd spend the weekend, if you don't mind."

"It's not up to me." The memory of the previous weekend, of Derrick in her bedroom, flashed through her mind. No. He wouldn't do that this weekend. He was trying to win her trust back. Besides, her bedroom in this house had a lock. "But I certainly don't mind."

His over-bright smile relaxed into one more natural. "Good. Tomorrow, you get the day off. I'll get up with Gramps, make sure he gets his meds, and you can sleep in."

Sleep in? She hadn't done that since she'd moved to Maryland. And hardly before that. But a morning off from work—she'd take that. "Sounds heavenly." She shooed him into the living room to visit with his grandfather. Then she put the flowers in a vase and ran upstairs to finish getting ready for their date.

She chose a red sundress he'd bought for her and added a pair of high-heeled sandals she'd picked up off the clearance rack. She added some lipstick and slid on a pair of earrings and a bracelet. She checked her reflection in the floor-length mirror in her private bath. Her outfit wasn't fancy, but it would be nice enough for wherever they went. Spending so much time in the garden with Red this week had given her a tan and lightened her hair. She looked summery, fancy-free. Maybe achieving the look would be a step toward achieving the feeling.

Downstairs, she went into the living room but found Red alone.

He whistled. "You look lovely."

She kissed his cheek. "Thank you."

"You mind Derrick spending the night?" Red asked.

"Not if you don't."

He nodded and turned his attention back to the TV.

A moment later, Derrick stepped into the room. "You ready?"

"Sure." To Red, she said, "Call me if you need me."

"I survived more'n eighty years without you, girl. I reckon I'll make it a couple of hours."

Harper settled into Derrick's car. "Can we stop at the store on the corner? I need to get some Gatorade."

"No problem." Derrick stopped, ran inside, and returned with a few bottles of yellow Gatorade. He tossed them in the backseat. "It's not like you to run out."

"Red worked in the yard all week. He was extra thirsty."

Derrick's eyes narrowed. "Should he be doing that?"

"He enjoys it. He's a grown man. It's not like I can tell him what to do. Besides, the sunshine was good for him, and I think the activity was, too."

"You're usually right about these things."

"Didn't he look good today? He's been so energetic all week."

Derrick exited the parking lot and headed toward the bay. "You've been good for him, Harper."

She shrugged. "I don't do much. I make sure he has his medication, make sure he eats, and encourage him to do his exercises."

Derrick glanced at her, then took her hand. "It's not what you do. It's who you are. You're a balm."

"Not really," she said, but her cheeks warmed with the compliment.

After a long wait with a crowd of tourists at the restaurant, they were seated on a covered patio overlooking a long dock and, beyond that, the sparkling waters of the bay. It was a warm night, but the breeze kept them cool. Every table was taken, and the buzz of conversation added to the gentle lapping of water and the caw of seagulls overhead.

Their conversation stayed on safe ground and far from the events of the previous weekend as they shared a delicious seafood dinner and chocolate dessert and sipped their drinks—sweet tea for Harper, a cold beer for Derrick. It was beautiful, the perfect night. And Derrick had been his old self. Sweet, generous, attentive. Maybe she could make things work with him. Maybe she'd made the right choice when she hadn't broken up with him the week before.

She glanced at him to see him not watching the view, but her.

He'd taken off his suit jacket and set it over the back of the chair when they'd sat. Now, he leaned over to reach something in the inside pocket. A moment later, he turned holding a thin rectangular box.

"Oh."

He smiled and handed it to her. "Open it."

Her hands trembled as she took the gift. She held it a long moment, trying to name the feeling that had her blood racing, her stomach flipping. It wasn't eagerness. It wasn't excitement or affection. Though she was eager to see the gift and thankful for it, something else caused her reaction.

Derrick was watching her, so she lifted the lid.

Inside, she saw a sapphire-and-diamond pendant on a slender gold chain.

She stared at the necklace, her hand covering her heart. She couldn't think of a word to say.

"The sapphire matches your eyes."

Sweet. Too much. She set the box down. "You didn't need to... You shouldn't have."

"I wanted to apologize for last weekend."

"You did apologize. On Sunday. And I forgave you."

"You're not one to hold a grudge." His smile faded. "Which is all the more reason I wanted to get you something."

"But..." She swallowed, put her hands in her lap, and ignored the jewels glimmering up at her from the tabletop. "You can't afford this, Derrick. You need every penny—"

"Don't do that." His lips flattened with the terse remark, turned white. "It's a gift. It's rude to refuse a gift."

"I'm not trying to be rude. I'm trying to... I don't understand why you would spend—"

"It's just a trinket."

"Oh." The satin-lined box looked fancy. But maybe it only *looked* expensive. Thank heavens. She blew out a breath. "It's not real. I'm glad, because—"

"Of course it's real." He sneered the last word. "You think I'd buy you some cheap, fake jewelry?"

Slowly, she replaced the lid and held the box out to him. "I think you're deeply in debt, and you can't afford to buy me anything."

He didn't take it. "Seriously? You're refusing it?"

She set the box on the table and turned toward the bay, thinking of what to say. A little crowd of seagulls had landed on the dock and were clawing and pecking at each other for a scrap of food.

Why did life have to be so hard?

She turned back to Derrick. "It was very sweet of you, and I love that you wanted to give me something."

His lips remained pressed closed, his eyes narrowed the tiniest bit.

"The thing is, if we remain together—"

"You say that like it's not likely." His words were harsh.

"Then we need to work as a team. People in a relationship should be on the same team, shouldn't they?"

His head angled just slightly to the side. "How is me giving you a gift showing that we're not on the same team?"

She shouldn't have started down this road. What did she know about sports? She'd never played a team sport in her life. But she knew how hard it was for people who weren't aiming toward the same goals to work together. She'd seen that tension at her first dancing job in Vegas. The showgirls had performed the same numbers while working toward their own selfish ambitions. Many had been cutthroat in their attempts to claw or sleep their way to the top. The only women who weren't that way had given up their dreams. They'd quit having any ambition at all. Together, the dancers had looked good on stage, but behind the scenes, the tension and drama had been cancerous. She'd hated it.

A relationship wasn't the same as a dance troupe, she knew. Or a sports team. But the analogy still worked.

"On a basketball team," she said, "everybody wants to win the game. Sometimes, that means one player passes the ball to another instead of taking a shot, because the other player has the better chance of scoring. Maybe that first person didn't get the applause, but that's not the reason they play. They play to win the game."

His eyebrows lifted, and he almost smiled. "I didn't know you were such a fan."

"I'm not, I'm just saying—"

"What does basketball have to do with a gift?"

"When two people care about each other, they work together to achieve their goals. They're on the same page. If one is trying to do something, the other helps."

"And in this case...?" he prompted.

"You need to pay off a debt, and I know that. I want us to work together. Which means, you don't waste money. Not even on me. And I understand that and support you. I don't expect"—she indicated the restaurant, the remnants of their pricey dinners, and the jewelry box—"fancy meals or fancy gifts or flowers. I'd be just as happy grabbing takeout and eating on a park bench."

She expected him to be pleased with her words. To find relief from the pressure of spending money on her. Instead, he snatched the gift and shoved it back in his jacket. "Fine."

"Why are you mad?"

"I'm not mad. I'm just..." But he didn't finish. When the waitress walked by, he asked for the check. He paid it, and they walked out of the restaurant in silence.

After they got in the car—he didn't open the door for her like he'd done before—he pulled away from the parking space and headed toward Red's house.

"Can you please just talk to me?" she asked.

"What do you want me to say? I bought you a nice gift, and you threw it in my face, along with all my faults and failures. All I wanted was to forget about my stupid crap for a little while. Is that so terrible?"

"If by 'forget' you mean you spend money you don't have, then maybe, yeah."

He took a deep breath. "I know what you're saying." The anger had drained from his voice. Now he just sounded defeated. "For the record, the necklace wasn't that expensive."

"For the record," she said, "it was beautiful."

He reached across the center console and took her hand. "I want to shower you with gifts."

"I don't need your gifts."

He lifted her fingers and kissed them gently. They were quiet until he pulled into Red's driveway. After Derrick slid the gear into Park and cut the engine, he took her hand again. "I hope, someday, you'll do more than just care for me."

She was forming an answer, but he continued.

"You're not there. I know. And I'm not pushing you. I'm just laying it out there. I know I said it the other night, but I was a little drunk and a little... Well, maybe not myself. So it was a lousy time to say it."

She knew what was coming and wished he wouldn't. But she'd already shut him down tonight with the necklace. She couldn't do it again.

"You're right about the team thing." He angled his shoulders to better face her. "I've never really been part of a team. What I do is dog-eat-dog. I played tennis in high school. Loved singles, hated doubles, because I hated having to depend on anyone else. I don't know how to be a teammate." He swallowed, looked beyond Harper. "Russell and Betts are a team. They're together in everything."

"They seem to be."

"It's beautiful. My parents weren't like that. They fought a lot." He focused on her again. "Anyway, it doesn't matter. I'm just saying, I want that someday. And not with just anybody." He leaned closer. "I love you, Harper. I hope someday you'll love me, too."

She didn't trust him nearly enough to consider anything deeper with him. But after he'd bared his soul, she couldn't very well say that. She placed her hand on his cheek and kissed him. "You're a kind man, Derrick Burns."

His chuckle was dark. "You might be the only person in the world who thinks so."

CHAPTER TWENTY-ONE

Harper finished reading her Bible before seven the next morning despite Derrick's suggestion that she sleep in. In her new life, she welcomed mornings. Nothing like her old, pre-prison life, which had thrived in darkness, drinking, and drugs.

She remembered one of the women who'd visited her in prison, a sweet Christian lady who ran the codependency group there. Whenever anyone would confess something particularly awful, she'd say, "Beautiful things only thrive in the light."

Harper was learning to thrive in the light.

It was Saturday, and again, clouds had moved in. She pitied all the folks who spent their weekdays trapped in office buildings, the people who yearned for sunny weekends. Based on her phone's weather app, they'd be disappointed today.

Since Derrick had promised to look after Red, Harper donned her running clothes and cheap tennis shoes, threw her hair into a ponytail, and stepped out of her room. She usually used the back staircase, which led straight to the kitchen, but she hoped to avoid Derrick and Red. There'd be plenty of time to visit later, and she didn't want to get pulled into a conversation that would keep her from her jog.

She shoved her phone in her shorts' pocket, just in case, and went down the stairs that led to the foyer. She was just about to open the door when she heard Derrick's voice in the kitchen.

What was he saying?

"Of course you wouldn't have to invest that much, but these stocks are supposed to go through the roof."

"And if they don't?" Red asked.

"It's what you've always told me. Make sure the investment is sound, do your homework. This company's numbers are good. They're making money. They're poised to take off. If they don't, it's not like you'll lose everything. You'll just have to wait it out."

"What kind of company is it again?" Red said.

"Tech. They build computer parts."

"Like Intel and Qualcomm?"

"Uh..." Derrick stumbled, obviously surprised to find Red so well informed. "Yeah, sort of."

What was going on? Derrick hadn't mentioned any investment to her. She'd heard nothing about it at the beach the previous weekend.

"How much do you need, son?" Red didn't sound eager or curious about the investment. Just tired.

"Whatever you want to invest." Derrick, on the other hand, sounded overly relaxed. Like it was all no big deal to him. He was good at that offhand tone. Very good. "But if I were you, I'd throw a couple hundred grand at it. I think the stock will double in the initial offering. Then, you can sell if you want, take your profit."

Harper looked at the front door, told herself she should go. What happened between Derrick and Red wasn't her business. Derrick was his grandson. She was just Red's nurse. And Derrick's girlfriend. Despite what she told herself, though, she tiptoed into the dining room, careful to stay out of sight.

Red blew out a long breath. "Let's cut the act. You're in over your head again, and you need me to bail you out."

"No, no," Derrick said. "It's not that. It's just this investment—"

"Where's the prospectus?"

"I forgot to bring it, but I can get you one."

"And you'd need me to make the check out to you?"

"Well..." Derrick cleared his throat. "I'm investing, and the more we put in, the better—"

"Listen, kid," Red said. "This ain't my first rodeo, and you're not the first desperate man who's tried to get money out of me. You forget, I was your father's father, and you're your father's son. I told you the last time I bailed you out I wasn't gonna do it again."

The chair scraped against the floor. Then she heard footsteps on the tile. "I'm not asking you to bail me out, Gramps. I'm trying to get you in on the investment of a lifetime."

"Hmph." Red was a lot sharper than Derrick gave him credit for. "Fortunately, I have all the money I need to last me until I leave this earth. So I'm going to skip your little investment."

"Fine."

Before she could react, footsteps stomped toward her. Derrick stepped into the dining room and froze when he saw her. His face was red, but the color faded as they stared at each other.

He continued past and bolted up the staircase.

Harper pasted on a smile and entered the kitchen. Red was seated at the table. The effects of his conversation with Derrick were etched on his face. "You on your way out?"

She glanced through the window at the cloudy day. "I was going to, but it looks like rain. I think I'll just stay here with you."

He nodded, nibbled his breakfast. Seemed Derrick had gone all out. Red had eggs and toast, not to mention a little bowl of assorted berries she'd picked up a few days before. He opened his newspaper and focused on the stories there.

She poured herself a cup of coffee, doctored it up, and got a bowl of fruit before joining Red at the table.

They sat in silence. The sound of Derrick pacing in his room upstairs was a frantic background beat. She was halfway through her coffee before Red spoke.

"How deep is he in?"

It wasn't her place to get involved. But Red wasn't stupid. "It's bad."

He folded the newspaper and set it down. His fingers rapped on the table.

She ate a blueberry, then a blackberry. The sweet of one mixed with the tart of the other and created a nice combination in her mouth, but she could hardly enjoy it.

Overhead, Derrick pounded on something. Probably his bureau.

"He's mad at me," Red said.

"It's not your problem."

"I told him the last time I bailed him out that it would be the *last time.*"

"Did he tell you it was an investment then, too?"

Red shook his head. "Just asked me for money. Twenty thousand. Not small potatoes, but this time... Two hundred? What did he do?"

Red didn't seem to want an answer, which was good, because Harper didn't have one.

"I did everything I could to help George." Red still didn't look at her. He was focused behind her, or maybe on events long past. "I bailed him out too many times before I said 'enough.' I thought if he knew I'd quit giving him money, he'd get his act together. They have those support groups, but he never went. Just blew every penny he had at the tables, and when I didn't help him, he mortgaged his house, his business. His wife was right there with him. She'd talk about how they needed to quit, but she was just as bad as he was. They'd gamble together, they'd win, all was well. They'd lose, and they'd fight." Red focused on Harper, his sharp blue eyes watery. "I knew better than to bail Derrick out. But the poor kid had lost his parents. He just had me, a grouchy old man. How do you do the tough-love thing in that situation? I got into the same stupid patterns with him. And now he's following the same path his father took."

"It's not your fault, Red. You know that, right?"

"Of course it's not my fault." His voice was sharp. "He didn't come to live with me until he was eighteen years old. The die had been cast long before that." He nibbled his toast, then set it down as if he was too drained to hold it up. "I sure wish I could've helped him, though."

The banging and pacing above quieted. She hated to think of how defeated Derrick must have felt. There'd be no easy way out of this situation for him.

Worse than that, she'd witnessed the whole thing. Witnessed him trying to swindle his own grandfather, this sweet, sweet man who'd done nothing but try to help him.

How desperate must Derrick be?

How low could a person fall?

She couldn't quantify the first and knew too much about the second.

They finished their breakfasts in silence. Red never glanced at the newspaper again. Poor man was worried. Heartbroken.

She knew how he felt.

Ten minutes later, Derrick's footsteps sounded on the stairs. She heard a thud, and then he stepped into the kitchen. "Something came up." He focused on his grandfather, avoiding Harper's gaze. "I'm headed back to the city."

Red nodded once. "Glad you came."

Derrick gave Red a pat on the shoulder.

He looked at Harper, and she stood and walked to the front door. She stopped beside Derrick's suitcase and turned to face him. Arms crossed.

He snatched the bag, opened the door, and stepped onto the stoop. She thought he was going to leave without a word, but instead, he held the door open. "Can we talk out here?"

She stepped into the muggy day.

He strode to his sedan, popping the trunk with his key fob halfway there. He tossed the suitcase in, then returned to the front step. He stopped a few feet from her and raked his fingers through his hair. "I don't know what to say."

"You're so desperate, you lied to your grandfather."

He crossed his arms. "You don't understand. I'm in trouble, Harper. These people—"

"How much is that car worth?"

"Not enough."

"It'd be a start, though."

"If I owned it, but I'm behind on my payments as it is."

"Could you refinance your condo?"

He swallowed. "I'll figure out something." He wore khakis and a golf shirt and looked like the successful young businessman she'd first thought he was. Nobody would ever know what he was capable of based on his looks. "I don't want this to come between us." Derrick stepped closer and reached for her hands.

She stepped back. "You're joking, right?"

His arms dropped. "Harper, I need you. And you need me."

"I just heard you try to con your grandfather out of two hundred thousand dollars."

His brown eyes lost their spirit, hardened until they looked like lifeless marbles. "It's not as if he doesn't have the money. He's loaded. He's got millions."

"Which he earned, Derrick. He spent a lifetime earning it."

"He got lucky in real estate." He stepped toward her again, and she backed up until she was pressed against the doorway. He was too close and too angry. "He gambled on real estate and won. But he looks down on me."

"Real estate and poker aren't the same."

"Whatever."

"Step back, Derrick."

"I need you. And you need me."

Was he crazy? "I don't need this."

He leaned closer, close enough to kiss her. She lifted her hands to block him, turned her head.

He didn't back up, just hovered, eyes hard.

She wanted to scream, to push him away.

A car door slammed down the street. The sound seemed to

bring Derrick to his senses. He took a step back. Blinked. His eyes were black as tar. "You're dumping me, after all I've done for you?"

There it was. Because he'd gotten her this job, she owed him.

Except it had been Red who hired her. Red who paid her. And it was Red who could be trusted. Not Derrick.

Definitely not Derrick.

"I don't owe you anything."

"Great. So I've lost my biggest client and the potential for another client—because of you."

He was delusional, but she kept her mouth shut.

"I lost big in poker that night because you wouldn't let me stay with you."

As if she ought to have slept with him to keep him from being an idiot. All that would have done was made her an idiot, too.

"I've lost Gramps. And to top it all off, you're dumping me."

"You should try taking responsibility for your own mistakes, Derrick. You'd be surprised how much better your life is when you realize you're in control of your own decisions."

"Said the felon."

Hot rage made her hands tremble. "It's time for you to go."

"You can't order me away from my own grandfather's house."

She crossed her arms and stood her ground. She lived here. Derrick didn't. End of story.

He stared at her, seemed to be waiting for her to back down. Well, he'd be waiting a long, long time.

Spitting a curse word, he spun, ran to his car, and peeled out of the drive.

She watched the street until long after he'd disappeared.

That was not how she'd planned for this day to go. She waited for some twinge of regret or remorse. All she felt was relief.

CHAPTER TWENTY-TWO

Ever since Derrick had tried to swindle him out of money a few months before, Red hadn't been the same. His moods shifted faster than the autumn weather, and she walked on eggshells around him. Sometimes, he was the happy-go-lucky guy she'd first met. Other times, he seemed so depressed she worried for his health. Still other times, he was angry, lashing out at her and anyone else within earshot.

She missed the sweet old man he'd once been. But she understood. Broken hearts were painful.

She'd thought he was getting better, but the grouch was back. "We have to go." Harper stood by Red's recliner, arms crossed.

"Don't feel like it."

She took a deep breath to silence her initial reaction. "As you've made perfectly clear, Red, but you're going to the doctor."

He ignored her, his gaze on the TV.

Today was his check-up, and he wasn't missing it. "Come on." She leaned toward the lever that would lower his footrest. "I'll help you—"

He swatted her arm away. "Don't need your help." He glared at her, then focused on the TV again.

Usually, when he got like this, she let him have his way. But not today.

"Listen, old man."

The anger dropped from his expression, replaced by surprise.

"You're going to the doctor on your own, or I'll call 911 and have them come after you."

"You wouldn't dare."

"Don't tempt me."

He harrumphed, glared, and finally lowered the footrest of his recliner. "Fine. But you can't make me talk to him."

Stubborn old coot. She grabbed his jacket—the October chill had settled deep—and helped him to the car.

An hour later, a nurse escorted Red back to the doctor's office. Harper had already updated the nurse on how he'd been feeling—and behaving—so Red's refusal to talk to them shouldn't make a difference. And they'd fill Harper in. Red had made her his health care agent when she'd started working for him. He'd ensured she'd have full access to all his medical information so she could learn what the doctors discovered whether Red was in the mood to tell her or not.

Amazing what a difference a few months had made. Back in Vegas, she hadn't been trusted to do anything but feed the residents and clean up after them. Here, she'd been given the right to make medical decisions. She'd proved herself to Red and, even though she barely spoke to him anymore, to Derrick. She hadn't gone back to school, hadn't achieved any real level of success, but maybe if her parents heard what she had achieved, they'd accept her again. Maybe if she told them where she was and what she was doing, they'd be proud of her. Or, if not proud, less ashamed. She considered dialing her mother that moment, but now wasn't the time. No, she needed to think about it some more. Being estranged from her parents was awful. A second rejection might destroy her.

Her cell vibrated, and she pulled it out and glanced at the screen. She had two missed calls and three texts from Derrick. She ignored them, as usual. He'd been trying to reconcile with her ever since he'd left her on the front stoop that stormy Saturday morning. At first, she'd been firm but kind. Now, she didn't bother to respond. They spoke sometimes about his grandfather's health. But Derrick hadn't been to visit him once since that terrible morning, despite that fact that she'd told Derrick about the mood swings and how she believed they were a direct result of Derrick not visiting.

Was he still angry at Red for not giving him the money? Was this some sort of manipulation technique? Did he think that if he withheld his love long enough, Red would give in? Or was he too busy trying to dig himself out of trouble—or maybe gambling himself into more debt—to bother with Red? She had no idea what was going on in Derrick's life and wouldn't care if his absence hadn't been such a blow to Red.

It was thirty minutes before a nurse called Harper back and into an empty exam room. "He seems as healthy as he can be at his age."

"But what about his moods?"

The woman shrugged. "He didn't complain of depression or mood shifts. He said he's fine."

Harper sighed. "He's just different than he used to be. More forgetful. What could cause that?"

"Old age affects everyone differently. The forgetfulness—that could be signs of dementia, but we saw nothing to suggest that today. He was a bit crankier than usual."

He was definitely that.

By the time she returned to the waiting room, Red was there, seated in a chair, arms crossed. He looked exhausted.

All this effort and no diagnosis. Poor man. She hoped this wasn't his age catching up with him. Prayed he wasn't deteriorating. She couldn't lose him. Red was the closest thing to family she'd had in years. She wasn't sure she'd survive without him.

CHAPTER TWENTY-THREE

That afternoon, after Harper got Red settled in his recliner, she went to the kitchen to warm up something for dinner. Soup tonight. It rarely disagreed with him, and even a totally incompetent cook—which she was—could heat a can of soup.

While it warmed on the stove, she poured Red a glass of Gatorade, took it out to him, and set it on his end table beside the photograph of his late wife. He'd already dozed off in the recliner. She hated to wake him to eat, but she would. He needed to take his medication, and he'd be extra cranky if he didn't eat. She set his glass on the end table and returned to the kitchen.

Much as she dreaded it, she needed to call Derrick.

She stirred the soup and dialed his number.

"Harper," he said, nearly breathless. "Thank God you called me back."

"It's about your grandfather."

A short pause, then, "Is he all right?"

"He's depressed."

"Why?" Derrick said. "What's he got to be depressed about?"

She silenced the sarcastic response. "He misses you."

"How about you?" Derrick's voice softened. "Do you miss me? Because I miss you. I need you."

Irritation rose like an itchy rash. "This isn't about you and me, Derrick. It's about Red. He hasn't laid eyes on you since you took off that day. Since you tried to—"

"I know what happened, Harper. I was desperate, okay? Don't you think I feel bad enough?"

Nope. She didn't, but she didn't say that. "You're not making it better by staying away. It's been months. You're the only family he has left. He needs to see you."

There was a long pause. She heard street noises in the background and wondered where he was. "You're right. I know you're right. I'm just... I'm ashamed of myself."

"Then apologize. He'll forgive you."

"But will you? Will you ever forgive me?"

She sighed, stirred the soup. "It's not a matter of forgiveness. It's about trust. I care for you, and I want what's best for you. But after what I saw with your grandfather, I don't trust you."

"But that's all taken care of now. I've made arrangements, and the debt'll be paid off soon."

She was in the middle of pulling a bowl down from the cabinet when she froze. Two hundred thousand dollars, and just like that, it was paid? "How?"

"The details don't matter. The point is, it's going to be managed."

"Did you gamble your way out of it?"

His short chuckle was dark. "Hardly."

"Then how—?"

"It's not your problem, and pretty soon, it won't be my problem, either. I've got it handled. And I quit gambling. For good, cold turkey. I'm done with it."

"Really?" Could that be true? Could Derrick really have done something so drastic, so quickly? "Are you going to meetings?"

"Don't need to. After I saw the way Gramps looked at me, and after you dumped me, I swore I'd never gamble again. And I haven't. Not since we went to the beach."

She was tempted, so tempted, to believe him. Because as certain as she'd been when she broke up with him that it was the right decision, she missed him. She missed the way he'd made her laugh, the way they'd dreamed of the future. She missed his attentiveness, the way he'd lavished her with tenderness. She missed the Derrick she'd met in Las Vegas. Maybe the real Derrick was the one she'd gotten to know at first. Maybe, without the gambling, he could be that man again.

"Give me another chance." His voice was quiet, pleading. "I need you."

There it was. His need. As if she could save him. As if his future were her responsibility. "I'm not ready for that yet. Maybe when your grandfather is himself again and you've been away from gambling longer, maybe then we can talk about it. Right now, let's just keep things as they are."

"As they are?" The tenderness had drained from his voice, and what replaced it confirmed her decision. "As in, we never see each other?"

"That's your choice, not mine. You know where to find me."

"Right. And I can visit you if I visit Gramps. But you don't want to date me. Or talk to me. You don't return my calls or my texts. You don't want anything to do with me."

She smelled something funny and realized the soup was bubbling in the pan. Crap. Only Harper could screw up soup. She yanked the pan off the burner and stirred. Bits of black came off the bottom.

"And now you're not even talking to me," Derrick said.

She dumped the soup and the scalding hot pan into the sink. Now what would they do for dinner?

"I guess I'll just hang up," he said.

Rage hotter than the soup rolled over her. "You know what, Derrick? Do whatever makes you happy. That's all you do anyway. Never mind your grandfather. Never mind that his heart is broken.

You keep having your little hissy fit because he wouldn't give you his money and I dumped you. One of these days, you're going to be planning his funeral, and then maybe you'll realize what you missed."

The pause that followed was so long, she thought he'd hung up. She was about do the same when she heard, "You're right."

"So you'll come to see him?"

"Yeah," he said. "I'll try to get up there this weekend."

CHAPTER TWENTY-FOUR

D errick didn't visit the following weekend. And he didn't visit the next, or the next. In fact, weeks went by, and they didn't hear from him.

Meanwhile, Red's moods didn't improve. They didn't get worse, either, so she decided to celebrate that.

The leaves changed, then dropped from the trees, but she and Red barely left the house to enjoy the cooler weather.

It was the first week of November, and Red was having a terrible day. He'd had a headache and been sick to his stomach all night. He'd skipped breakfast but had eaten a decent lunch. After he ate, he slept in his recliner all afternoon. Odd. She wondered if he was fighting a virus.

They were in the kitchen, Harper cleaning up from their dinner, when he slammed his glass on the table. "Bring me more Gatorade!"

She set down the dishrag, propped her hands on her hips, and glared at him. "I'm sorry. What did you say to me?"

"More"—he lifted his empty glass and shook it in her direction —"this stuff."

His words were slurred as if he were drunk.

And then he vomited all over his plate.

She rushed to his side, unbuttoned his soiled shirt, and slipped it off of him, leaving him shivering in the T-shirt beneath. She cleaned his hands and his mouth and helped him stand. "Come on. Let's get you into your recliner."

He could hardly get himself up. When he did, he swayed against his walker—a new addition he'd railed against when the doctor had suggested it. She steadied him and kept him from falling.

She managed to get him into his chair. He muttered something that sounded like thank-you.

She took his hands. "Squeeze my fingers."

He looked at her as if she were crazy but did as he was told. His grip was strong.

"Lift your hands above your head."

"What the devil—?"

"Just do it, please?"

He held his arms out horizontally, then lifted them up high. "Touchdown."

She chuckled politely. Hmm. His muscles were working fine. She lifted three fingers in front of his face. "How many?"

"Three." The word was strong and certain.

She snatched a pen off his end table. "Track it with your eyes." She moved in slowly in front of his face, and he followed it perfectly.

"What's my name?"

"Harper Cloud."

Right answer, but slightly slurred.

"Why am I here?"

"You're my nurse, though right now, I think you've gone a bit nuts."

"What's your favorite kind of nut?"

He narrowed his eyes, seemed to be formulating a wise crack, and then sighed. "Cashews."

Yup. The man ate them like candy. "What's your name?"

"Harold Carlock Burns. But everybody calls me Red."

She took his blood pressure. It was normal, if anything, a little low.

Perching in the chair beside him, she tried to think what could cause slurred speech. Aside from that, there were no signs of stroke.

"I'm thirsty," he said.

"You just threw up."

His eyes widened. "I did?"

He'd forgotten?

"I'm still thirsty."

She went into the kitchen, poured him a glass of Gatorade, and took it out to him.

He guzzled it.

"Slow down. You're going to be sick again."

But he ignored her and focused on the TV, the glass cradled in his hand.

If she didn't know better, she'd say he was drunk. She pulled a blanket over him and sat beside him until he fell asleep. It took him less than three minutes.

After she cleaned up the mess in the kitchen, she called the doctor's office and got a nurse on the phone. Harper described the symptoms, and the nurse confirmed that it was probably a virus. "If he continues to throw up or starts refusing to drink, you'll need to bring him in. Otherwise, let's just wait it out a couple of days."

Wait it out. That would be a good idea, except Harper couldn't silence the niggling thought that this was something serious.

Could his health fail this fast?

She'd seen it happen, of course. In the nursing home where she'd worked, she'd seen people go from relatively healthy to very sick to the grave in a matter of weeks, sometimes days. But there was always a reason. The flu or a virus could lead to pneumonia. A fall could result in a broken bone, which could be the first domino that ultimately led to death.

But in Red's case, what had been the catalyst? This virus

couldn't be blamed. He'd only been sick a few days. But his health, his moods, his depression...

The only thing that had changed was Derrick's behavior. Could all this be the result of a broken heart?

Did Derrick care at all?

Yeah, Derrick cared. About the money Red hadn't given him. About his inheritance.

The thought shamed her. How could she think such a thing? Derrick loved his grandfather. He was angry Red hadn't given him money, but that didn't change the underlying love the two men had for each other. Derrick was just desperate, and desperate people did desperate things.

Which was why, the week after Derrick had tried to swindle Red out of money, Red had asked his lawyer and friend, Roger, to come by. They'd drawn up some sort of papers that would give Roger power of attorney in case something happened to him. The paperwork also protected Red's money, in case Derrick should try to swindle him again. Essentially, it gave Roger the right to appeal any large distributions of cash. She hadn't been in their meeting, of course, and didn't know the details, only that if Derrick came back with any tall tales that involved large sums of money, she was supposed to call Roger.

Red's money was safe. But Derrick hadn't come back.

So much for all his promises.

And now, Red was sick. She should call Derrick and tell him, but she knew where that would lead. Absolutely nowhere. Besides, it was Thursday. Derrick wouldn't make the drive from Baltimore until the weekend unless there were an emergency. If things didn't change, she'd call him tomorrow.

From the living room, Red shouted, "Bring me a drink!"

She snatched his cup and poured the last of the yellow-green liquid into it. It only filled halfway, so she stepped into the garage where she kept the case of Gatorade she'd bought a few weeks before.

Red hollered again. "Thirsty!"

What in the world? This demanding tone was not like him. A virus couldn't make him mean, could it?

She returned to the kitchen and twisted the top of the Gatorade. It opened easily. Far too easily.

She lifted the bottle. It looked fine. It probably was fine. Did Gatorade go bad? Did it ferment?

No. Surely not.

But maybe that would explain the vomiting. Had the last bottle been easy to open? She couldn't remember.

Well, she wasn't taking any chances with Red's health. She returned to the garage, snatched another bottle from the case, and looked at the seal.

It was broken. The bottle had been opened. She twisted off the cap and sniffed it. It smelled like Gatorade. She looked at the yellow liquid. It looked like Gatorade. She took a sip. It tasted like Gatorade.

What in the world?

She hefted the other three bottles that remained in the case into the kitchen. All of them had been opened. Had they spoiled?

Sheesh. The store manager was going to get a piece of her mind when she went back. If that's what caused Red's illness, they were going to get a lot worse than that.

"I'm thirsty!" Red yelled.

She forced a deep, calming breath, then went into the living room. "We're out of Gatorade."

"There's a whole case out there."

"I think it went bad. I think that's why you're sick."

"Gatorade doesn't go bad." He winced, held his head. "My head is pounding."

She returned to the kitchen, grabbed two Tylenols and a glass of sweet tea, and took them to him."

"I want my Gatorade."

"We're out."

He snatched the pills, drank the tea, and scowled. "Don't like this stuff."

"I can get you water, if you'd prefer."

He started to say something, paused, and focused on the TV. "Sorry I've been so mean to you."

"Oh." She hadn't expected that. "You don't feel good."

When he focused on her again, she saw the sweet, gentle man who'd been there all along. "It scares me, you know?" His words were a little slurred. Again, she had the thought that if she didn't know better, she'd think he were drunk. "I'm afraid I'll never feel good again."

She set her hand on his bony shoulder. "You will. I'm sure you will."

He rested his head against the chair. "I'm gonna take a little nap. Will you get me more Gatorade?"

She considered it, but... "I don't want to leave you alone."

He patted the house phone, which was never very far. "Your phone number is programmed in here. Number three."

"That's right."

"I'll call you if anything happens. You can just run to the grocery store. You'll be gone, what, thirty minutes?" He closed his eyes. "What can happen in thirty minutes?"

She didn't want to leave him alone, but she needed him to stay hydrated and knew he'd dig his heels in about Gatorade. "You promise you won't try to stand?"

He didn't even open his eyes when he answered. "Scouts honor."

Fine. She kissed his forehead. "I'll be right back."

CHAPTER TWENTY-FIVE

Harper snatched the keys to Red's Cadillac and headed out. She'd be happy to drive her Jetta, but Red and Derrick had both insisted that she use the Caddy as long as she was staying at the house. Which made sense—her Jetta was so old, it could die at any moment, and she needed a car she could rely on. So her old VW had been parked in the two-car garage for months.

The dark sedan that was so often parked in front of the house further down the street wasn't there. Even though she knew it was nothing to worry about, she was glad to see the spot empty. For some reason she never understood, that car made her skin crawl. Old habits. If nothing else, at least she was safe in Maryland. Eventually, her heart would believe it.

It was dark by the time she wheeled her grocery cart out of the store. She'd grabbed six bottles of Red's favorite flavor, lemon-lime. She checked her watch—she'd been gone twenty minutes already. She should have had the Gatorade delivered. She hadn't considered it until she'd stepped into the grocery store and seen the sign advertising home delivery. She'd never used it, relishing her trips away from the house, enjoying the change of scenery. Today, she hurried and told herself Red was fine. Asleep. And he'd still be asleep when she returned. Alive and snoring softly in his chair.

But her stomach filled with acid anyway.

And her skin crawled.

Paranoia, nothing more.

The parking lot was about a third full of cars but empty of shoppers and store employees at the moment. She stopped the cart beside the trunk of Red's Caddy, then walked to the door and pulled it open. She tossed her keys and purse onto the seat and popped the trunk.

"Harper?"

She whipped around, startled.

On the other side of the open door stood a man.

He wore a ski mask.

She opened her mouth to scream, but from behind her a hand clamped over her face, and an arm wrapped around her waist.

She struggled silently, uselessly.

The person holding her pulled her from behind the open door. He pressed her against his body.

The masked man slowly pushed her door closed. He wore dark jeans and a black wool jacket over a black turtleneck. It was too dark to see the color of his eyes or skin. His hair was completely covered. Only his lips showed through the hole in the mask.

He leaned in close. She thought he was going to say something, but he didn't speak. Just nuzzled his nose against her neck. His breath sent a shudder of terror through her, and she lifted her shoulder to block him from touching her. The man behind her yanked her head to the side.

The masked man inhaled her scent, then chuckled.

A deep, rumbly sound from the pit of hell.

He shifted, but she couldn't see what he was doing. The man behind her held her head too tightly. She heard a snap. Caught sight of a blade and squeezed her eyes closed. *Oh, God, help!*

The cold edge sliced across her neck. The cut burned, and a warm trickle dribbled toward her collarbone.

She was going to die. One more inch, and the blade would slice her jugular.

And then the blade was gone.

She opened her eyes, saw the man's face just inches from hers. His hot finger slid down her neck in a perversely gentle move. Again, she struggled away from his touch, and again, the man behind her held her still.

The man lifted his finger so she could see her blood, then wiped it on his jeans. Through that small opening for his mouth, she saw him smile.

Then he punched her in the stomach.

The breath whooshed out, and her legs buckled.

The other man lost his hold over her mouth, but it didn't matter. She couldn't get enough air to scream. He kept her upright, and the other man backhanded her in the face.

She crumpled to the ground, curled into the fetal position, and covered her head with her arms.

One of them grabbed her arm and yanked her back. Pain shot through her wrist, but still, she had no air to scream.

The other man grabbed one of her legs. They pulled until she was lying flat out and helpless on the asphalt.

They flipped her on her stomach.

She reached forward, desperate to crawl away, to slide beneath the car, to make it all stop. Her hand touched something, and she grabbed it, held on, before she realized it was one of the men's shoes. She recoiled as if she'd touched a rattlesnake.

One of them stomped a foot between her shoulder blades, and the little air she'd been getting was forced out.

The other dragged her in front of her car so she was hidden between hers and the one parked in front. She could feel him looking down at her, watching her.

She curled up, covered her head. Tried to pray but couldn't seem to form anything beyond, *please, please.*

She still couldn't get breath to scream.

She heard movement. Heard her trunk close. Heard the shopping cart being rolled away.

The man standing over her bent down, whispered in her ear, "Tell him we stopped by."

Then they were gone.

CHAPTER TWENTY-SIX

H arper worked to pull air into her lungs until her breathing was normal again.

They were gone. She was alone. Still, she didn't move.

Cold from the asphalt seeped through her jeans, soothed the pain in her right wrist. A shopping cart wheeled past. She told herself to rise but didn't. Because if the people walking by were good people, they'd call the police, who'd want her to answer a bunch of questions. She had no information to give them. No idea what the attackers had been driving or what they looked like. There was nothing the police could do for her. They'd just slow her down.

Red. She had to get back to Red.

When the noises faded, she sat up, took a deep breath.

The cold air revived her.

Using the front fender for help, she pulled herself to a standing position. Her back ached from where the man had stomped it, but she could move. It was only bruised, nothing worse.

She twisted her right wrist in every direction. Painful, but it wasn't broken. Just a sprain.

Tentatively, she touched her cheek and winced.

It hurt, but she was fine. She inhaled another deep breath of that sweet, sweet oxygen and made it to the driver's door.

She was fine. She'd be fine.

She grabbed her keys and purse from the seat, slid in, then slammed the door and locked it.

She was safe. For now.

Only then did she begin to tremble.

She glanced at the clock on the dash. Thirty minutes had passed since she'd walked out of the grocery store.

Two for the assault, twenty-eight for her to drag herself to her car. Not very good numbers.

She used to be so much tougher than that.

What if Red had woken, gotten confused? Her heart pounded a rapid-fire rhythm. She had one job—take care of Red. What if she'd blown it tonight? What if something happened to him while she was gone trying to help him?

All this for Gatorade.

She backed out of the spot and hurried to the mansion she'd had the gall to call home.

Ten minutes later, she pulled to a stop in the garage, hit the remote to close the garage door, and popped the trunk. Before she exited the car, she checked her reflection in the rearview mirror. She was pale, but no bruises had formed. She angled so she could see her neck. The cut was angry and red, and a trail of blood led to her golf shirt. She lifted the collar to hide it and pushed open the door.

She lifted one foot and set it on the concrete floor, then turned to get the other out. The motion sent a shot of pain through her upper back. She breathed through it, shifted until she was facing out, and stood.

So far, so good.

It seemed that if she kept her back straight, didn't twist or bend, it was fine. Walking as stiffly as possible, she made her way to the trunk. It was crazy to think her attackers had loaded the bottles for her, but something had been rolling around in there on the drive back.

She peeked inside, and there were the drink bottles.

What kind of attackers...?

The professional kind. The kind who attacked because it was their job, though that man's smile...

She shook it off, bent at the knees, and managed to pull out one bottle. She carried it into the house and set it on the counter. Then she moved as fast as she could into the living room.

Red woke with a start, glared at her. "Where's the fire?"

The anxiety she'd been holding whooshed out. She turned off the lamp on the table beside him, sat on the couch, and stared at the stupid game show on the screen. He was fine. Nothing had happened.

Not to him, anyway.

The room was dim, soothing with just the one small lamp on. Dim was good. Dim meant Red, with his failing eyesight, wouldn't be able to see her well.

His chair creaked, and the footrest on his recliner slid back beneath the seat. She turned to find him looking at her. His scowl was gone. Somehow, so was the strange behavior from earlier. He seemed normal. Like a drunk who sobered up in a crisis. "You okay?"

For the first time since the assault, tears filled her eyes. She sniffed, nodded. "I'm fine."

"What happened?"

"I... I slipped and fell in the parking lot at the grocery store." She pulled the collar up on her shirt, just in case. "Landed on my back."

He reached across the space and took her hand. The strength of his grip always surprised her. "Should we go to the ER?"

"No, no. It's nothing. Just a bruise." She wiped the few tears, met the old man's eyes, saw kindness and concern there, which only made her want to cry more. She squeezed his hand. "I'm fine, really. I got your Gatorade."

He still watched her, his eyes piercing as if he could see through her lies. "You sure they aren't back?"

"They who?"

"Whoever..." The slur returned to his voice, and he waved his hands toward her. "Whatever it is puts that haunted look in your eyes. Makes you jumpy."

"Oh." He was more perceptive than she'd realized. "There's nobody. Just my own silly fears."

He studied her a minute more before he nodded. "Just sit with me and rest. Okay?"

She smiled and sat back in the chair.

A few minutes passed, and Red shifted his focus to Pat Sajak and Vanna White on the screen.

As much as she'd like to get lost in the puzzle on TV, Harper had a call to make.

"I'll be right back." She stood carefully, returned to the kitchen, and fixed him a glass of Gatorade. After she set it on the end table beside him, she returned to the kitchen and pulled her cell phone from her purse. She was still trembling.

Derrick answered after the second ring. "Hey." His voice was tentative. "Is Gramps all right?"

"I need you to come right away."

"Is he sick?"

She told herself not to analyze the tone of his voice, but the word *hopeful* sprang to mind. "He's fine, but we have an emergency. How soon can you be here?"

"This time of night... Probably forty-five minutes. I'm on my way."

After she hung up, she returned to the living room and watched TV with Red, careful of the sharp pains in her back. They were already better than they had been. After a night's sleep, she'd be good as new. Red was quiet, dozing. If not for the strange illness, he'd be studying her, trying to figure out what was going on with her. Even healthy, he'd never guess in a million years that she'd been assaulted. Funny how something so life-altering could be so easily hidden. Shoved to the back-burner. Forgotten. As if having her life threatened were nothing noteworthy. As if having strangers capture her, attack her, and leave her writhing in pain on the pavement were no big deal.

But she knew better. Knew the two minutes tonight in the parking lot would plague her for a long time.

Finally, a soft knock at the front door was followed by the sound of the key sliding into the lock. The door opened, and she walked through the formal dining room and met Derrick in the foyer. She stayed on the far side, crossed her arms. In the dim light, she saw the man she'd nearly fallen for. The brown hair with its widow's peak hairline, the kind hazel eyes and glasses that made him look geeky and kind. Everything about Derrick seemed normal, down-to-earth, gentle. She should have known better.

He looked at her, blinked, stepped closer. "What happened?"

"Quite a few things, actually."

He flipped on the chandelier. "Are you bleeding?"

She pulled her collar up to hide the cut. "Not anymore."

He reached toward her. "Let's go sit down. Is Gramps okay?"

She stepped back, out of his reach. "Go out to the Caddy and grab the Gatorade from the trunk. Please. Then we'll talk."

"Uh..."

She stepped into the half bath off the foyer, wet a tissue, and dabbed at the dried blood that had left a track along her skin. Thank God Red hadn't seen the cut. She added some antibacterial lotion and a bandage, then returned to the kitchen, where Derrick was setting down the bottles of Gatorade he'd carried in.

"It's not like you to run out of Gatorade. You want them in the garage?"

"Set them on the counter."

He did, then they both sat at the table. The light was brighter here than it had been in the foyer, and when he sat, he studied her. "Geez, Harper. What happened?" He reached out like he might touch her face, the red spot she'd barely glanced at in the bathroom. She leaned back, and he dropped his hand on the table.

"You're saying you don't know?"

"How would I?"

Based on the confusion on his face, he had no idea. But she'd quit believing anything Derrick said. He reached for her hand, and she jerked away.

Pain shot through her upper back, and she froze, breathed through it.

Derrick lowered his hand. "You're hurt. I need to take you—"

"You've done enough, I think."

His eyes narrowed. He leaned back just enough. "What are you talking about?"

"Have you had someone watching me?"

"Of course not. Why would I?"

Either he was the best liar in the world—and that was entirely possible—or he had no idea. Still...

"They told me to tell you they stopped by."

The color in his face faded. "Who?"

"The men who did this to me."

"Men?" He leaned toward her. "What men? Where were you?"

"This was about you."

"I don't know why someone would—"

"I assume they were trying to send you a message," she said. "Maybe if you'd let them know we broke up—"

"No, Harper. This wasn't... Whatever happened, it didn't have anything to do with me. I don't know what you're talking about."

"So you know nothing about the men who beat me up in the grocery store parking lot?"

He reached across the table. When she didn't take his hand, he left it there, palm up, an invitation she'd never accept. "Please, start at the beginning."

The memory of it had her rubbing her wrist. He caught the motion. "Here, let me—"

"No. You don't get to cause this and then comfort me. Whatever's going on with your goon friends, tell them we're not together anymore."

He stared at her with that fake innocence. She couldn't stand to look at him. "Go see Red. He misses you."

"I don't know what's going on."

"You still owe people money?"

His expression gave away nothing. After a moment, he nodded.

"I thought you said it was taken care of."

"I'm working on it."

"Apparently, it's time to renegotiate your payment plan."

His head dropped forward. He dug his fingers in his hair and kept his face hidden for a long time. When he looked up, his eyes were red, worried. "I'm sorry. I don't know what's going on. I'll... I mean, if this had anything to do with me, then I'll see what I can do."

"Unless your grandfather is into shady business, Derrick, it has to be about you."

He swallowed, nodded. "You're probably..." Tears filled his eyes, but he didn't look away. "I would never hurt you. You have to know that."

But he had hurt her. A lot.

"I'm trying to fix it. I'm going to get it fixed. I still haven't gambled. And I haven't come by because I wanted to be able to tell you that it was all taken care of. I thought it would be, sooner than this. But things just... Nothing seems to work out for me."

Wow. She'd been assaulted tonight, and he had the nerve to feel sorry for himself. She couldn't even muster the anger he deserved.

"Go see your grandfather."

Derrick stood. "It's late. I'll visit this weekend."

She stared at this man she'd thought she might someday love. "I keep thinking you might surprise me. You might turn into the man I thought you were when I first met you." She stood. "Don't make promises you don't intend to keep."

"I never meant for you to get hurt. I love you, Harper." He wiped a few tears from his eyes.

The tears were authentic, but they weren't for her. He didn't love her. She wasn't sure what love was, but it wasn't this. It wasn't lies and manipulation and broken promises.

"I know I should have come sooner," he said. "It's just... It's hard to be here with us like"—he indicated the space between them —"like this."

She closed her eyes. "Just get out."

CHAPTER TWENTY-SEVEN

Somehow, Harper got through the rest of the evening. She'd been careful to keep her collar pulled up high to hide the bandage on her neck as she'd given Red his last round of medication. He drank his Gatorade and already seemed to feel better. After he finished his nighttime routine, she helped him into his room.

"I can put myself to bed, you know," he said. "I'm not a two-year-old."

She pulled the covers up to his neck. Normally, she'd lean down to kiss his forehead, but her back wouldn't like that. And if she leaned too much, he'd have a great view of her neck, and she didn't have the energy to deflect his questions right now. She patted his shoulder. "I want to tuck you in, you grouchy old coot."

He gripped her hand. "If your back's not better tomorrow, we're going to the doctor."

She didn't bother to argue. Sick as he was, he'd probably forget by morning.

After Harper closed his bedroom door, she checked all the doors and windows. Everything was locked.

Those goons had sent their message, and she'd passed it along. She was safe now.

Why was she always trying to convince herself of that?

All the events of the previous few hours came back, and her hands trembled again. She made it to her bedroom and locked the door. She kept the light off and peeked through the blinds out the window. The sedan that was parked in front of the neighbors' house so often was gone.

Had Derrick been watching her? It didn't make sense, but then, what did? The only people she knew in Maryland, the only people she knew on the East Coast, were Derrick, Red, Roger, Red's lawyer, the folks she'd met at the beach, and Red's many healthcare providers. So who would watch her?

And why?

All this time, she'd thought she was being paranoid, told herself the car was owned by the people who lived in that house. But she'd never seen anyone get in or out. She'd never seen it pull up to the house, either. It was almost always there after dark. From here, she'd never been able to see if anybody was inside the car. There'd just been that one time when she'd been sure she saw the glow of a cell phone.

She sighed and let go of the blinds. After tonight, she wasn't about to pass off her fear as paranoia. Tonight, her suspicion felt justified.

Red's illness had exhausted her. The attack... She didn't want to think about that. She didn't want to think about anything.

She went into her private bathroom and locked that door, too. She turned on the shower. While it warmed up, she undressed and looked at herself in the mirror. There'd be an ugly bruise on her cheek in the morning. She hoped makeup would cover it so Red wouldn't notice. They'd have to stay close to home the next few days until it faded. She removed the bandage and studied the cut on her neck again. It was ugly, but it wasn't deep. She could wear turtlenecks until it healed. Her stomach and ribs ached, but nobody could tell that from looking at her.

A bruise was forming on her wrist. Fortunately, it was cold enough for long sleeves.

She turned to look at her upper back but saw no shoe print there. As usual, the worst blows left no visible marks.

She had enough experience to know invisible scars could twinge for years.

She turned and met her gaze in the mirror. "You're fine. You've lived through worse."

She stepped into the shower, let the hot water wash away the memories, the feel of that man's hand over her mouth, the other man's breath on her neck.

Her tears fell, mingled with the water, left her feeling, if not clean, at least cleansed of the evil men she'd encountered that night. The attackers. And Derrick.

When the tears were spent, she breathed deeply of the humid air, let even her lungs be washed of memories so she could think straight.

If only she hadn't gone out for Gatorade. If only the Gatorade bottles hadn't already been opened. That a grocery store had let...

Wait. The case had been wrapped in plastic when she'd bought it. The bottles couldn't have been opened before that unless the person who'd opened them had had some way to rewrap them in plastic. But what would have been the point? It was just a handful of bottles. Worth, what, ten dollars? Why go to all that trouble?

Nobody would have done that. Which meant that the bottles had been opened after she'd gotten them home.

But who? Not Red. The only other person who had access to the house was Derrick, and he hadn't been there in months.

Or had he?

She'd kept the Gatorade in the garage. He wouldn't have even had to come in the house. He could have tampered with them out there, and nobody would have known. He could slip in and out without anybody knowing.

No. What was she saying?

It was insane.

And yet... Derrick was desperate.

She didn't want it to be true, but by the time the hot water faded to warm, by the time she turned off the spigot and dried off, she knew she needed to call the police. If those bottles had been tampered with, the police needed to know.

And she should report the attack as well. She'd been foolish not to.

Decision made, she dried off and was wrapping her wet hair in a towel when she heard a door slam.

Her heart pounded. It was probably just Red going to the bathroom. Based on the adrenaline rush to her veins, her heart wasn't convinced.

She slipped on her bathrobe, grabbed her can of mace out of her purse—her keychain with the knife was downstairs by the door —and stepped into the hallway outside her room. Red's bedroom was on the far end of the hall. His door was open. She peeked. He wasn't in bed. She looked into his attached bath. Empty.

She swallowed a rise of panic.

Normally, she'd call for him, but the memories of the evening were too close, whispering like ghosts in her ear. She tried to tamp down her fear as she stepped silently down the back staircase.

She made it to the kitchen, but Red wasn't there.

She transferred the pepper spray to her left hand, finger on the trigger, and grabbed a knife from the block on the counter.

Quietly, she crossed the tile and tiptoed into the living room.

Red was standing beside his recliner, one hand resting on the back of it, staring at the floor on the far side of the sofa. Sick as he was, how in the world had he gotten downstairs? Was he sleepwalking? What was he staring at?

She forced herself to speak calmly and said, "Red? Is everything okay?"

He looked at her, didn't seem to recognize her, and looked back at the floor.

What was that in his eyes? A look she'd never seen before on his face.

Terror.

She stepped closer and followed his gaze.

Two men were lying on the floor. She focused on one. Saw jeans and black turtleneck and black wool coat. There was a dark stain on the jeans. A bloodstain. Her blood. The ski mask was gone.

The other man... Her breath hitched. It was Kitty's husband, Keith Williams.

These were the men who'd attacked her.

She didn't have to take a pulse to know they were dead.

One look at their foreheads confirmed that. Bullet holes.

CHAPTER TWENTY-EIGHT

Harper couldn't make herself move.

This wasn't happening. This couldn't be happening.

Something gripped her arm, and she jumped and twisted. Pain shot up her back. She breathed through it while she stared at Red's bewildered gaze.

She slid the knife and pepper spray into the pocket of her bathrobe. Red wasn't holding a gun. Of course he wasn't. He couldn't have done this.

She gripped his upper arm. "Come on." She helped him into the kitchen, where she settled him in a chair. How had he gotten so far without his walker? Adrenaline. Fear could do that to people, give them strength they hadn't known they had. Eventually, the strength would run out, and they'd be left weaker, more vulnerable, than ever.

His face was pale, his hands trembling. She knelt in front of him. "What happened?"

He only shook his head.

"Did you see anything? Was someone here?"

His gaze flicked to her. Behind his eyes, she saw nothing but confusion. This time of night, considering how sick he'd been all day, considering what he'd just seen... He'd checked out. He probably wouldn't remember any of this in the morning. It was one of the reasons Derrick had insisted he needed a private nurse—these sporadic moments of forgetfulness

He'd be no help.

She checked the doors. The one leading to the garage was still dead-bolted, as was the front door. The door that led to the back patio wasn't fully closed, even though she knew she'd bolted it earlier. She didn't touch it. Maybe there'd be fingerprints or something.

She should call the police.

She turned, saw the bodies again. Keith. Kitty's husband. A loan shark's goon. Also, a detective. A cop. Dead in the house where she'd been living.

She had to force herself to take deep breaths, to think.

She returned to the kitchen, where Red was staring at the wall, half asleep but safe. For now.

Who'd killed those men? And why leave them here?

Was someone trying to frame her? With her record, she'd be the perfect person to frame for murder. But for what purpose? What threat did she pose to anyone? All she did was care for...

The bottles of Gatorade she'd just bought caught her eye.

If her suspicions were right, then somebody was trying to kill Red. Maybe that same someone wanted her out of the way to get to Red's money. The most obvious person who'd benefit from Red's death was Derrick. Would he have killed these men?

She couldn't imagine. The man she'd known would never be capable of such violence, of such evil. On the other hand, the man she'd known had never truly existed.

But to frame her? Why would he do that, when he'd been trying to get her back for weeks? Just today, he'd told her he loved her. Was that all a lie? For what purpose?

And why leave the bodies here?

Was it a threat? Were she and Red in danger?

Obviously they were. A murderer had left two bodies in this house. And Harper didn't know why.

A murderer. In her house.

Fear skittered down her back, and she looked around. She patted Red on the hand and began to search. She was sure the murderer was gone. But what if he wasn't?

She made sure the door to the garage was dead-bolted. Then she pulled her mace and the knife she'd grabbed earlier from the pockets of her bathrobe. Her hands trembled as she held her weapons in front of her and crept through the house, a scream trying to claw its way up her throat. The pantry, the half-bath, the front closet, Red's office—all empty. In the living room, she kept her gaze away from the dead men and looked behind the sofa. She crept upstairs, searched Derrick's room—his since his parents had died—the guest room, and Red's room. Then her own room, just in case.

She grabbed her cell phone. An intelligent person would've called the police immediately. Or just jumped in the car and run.

She wasn't making very logical decisions.

She returned to the kitchen, certain the house was empty of bad guys. For now. Red was dozing in the hard-backed kitchen chair.

She sat beside him and returned to the question she'd been mulling before the sudden search. Who else would benefit from Red's death?

The people Derrick owed money to. If Derrick inherited Red's estate, he'd be able to pay them back. Was that how this kind of thing worked?

It didn't make sense.

And until she understood why the men had been murdered and left there, how could she call the police? She'd be in jail before the sun came up. And then where would Red go? To a nursing home? Or would the police hand him over to Derrick? Derrick, who may be trying to kill him.

Could Red's attorney get involved? Would he believe her if she told him Derrick had been poisoning Red? How could she trust Roger when she barely knew him?

And how could she trust the police to protect Red? She'd trusted the police before, and she'd paid for that decision with two years in a state penitentiary.

With a dead cop thrown into the mix... They'd be ruled by emotions, not logic. They wouldn't care about some sick old man. They'd only care about finding the killer. And they'd look at her first. With Red's dementia, they wouldn't trust his accounting of her whereabouts tonight. Red wouldn't be able to tell them what time she'd gone to bed. He wouldn't be able to convince them she'd been home all evening. And she hadn't been. She'd gone out for Gatorade. Would they use that against her?

The only person who could corroborate her alibi wouldn't be fit to testify.

Her reason for going out wouldn't make sense to anyone. Why buy more bottles of what you already had?

But she could explain. She could prove it—show them the bottles of Gatorade. She rushed to the garage to grab one of the bottles, to keep it for evidence.

But the Gatorade that had been there, the Gatorade she'd thought poisoned, was gone.

Derrick must have taken them. Which proved her theory—he'd poisoned his grandfather.

Prison. She'd end up back in prison.

She returned to the kitchen, collapsed into a chair, and squeezed her eyes closed. She'd survived prison before. She could survive again. But Red...

Somebody had planted the bodies there for a reason, and Harper had no idea what that reason was. A threat? An attempt to frame her? Something else?

All she knew was that she didn't know anything. She certainly didn't know whom she could trust. Not the police. Not Derrick. Not anybody.

Just herself.

She had to keep Red safe. That was her first priority. And then she had to figure out what was going on. Maybe if the police found the bodies, they'd investigate and discover who the real killers were. Or maybe, if she had enough time, she could do some research, figure it out herself. Then, she could come back.

But right now, she and Red had to go.

CHAPTER TWENTY-NINE

Harper left Red in the kitchen and rushed upstairs. She snatched his suitcase from his walk-in closet and filled it with his favorite clothes and a spare pair of shoes. After she tossed in all his toiletries and medications, she rushed into her room. Her suitcase was falling apart, but she'd make it work. She grabbed all the clothes and toiletries she could fit into it. Warm things, comfortable things. The gifts Derrick had given her—clothes, shoes, jewelry—she left.

Careful of her back, she carried the suitcases downstairs and hefted them into the trunk of her beat-up VW Jetta. The Caddy was better in every way except one: its navigation software would make her far too easy to track. The Jetta would blend in and keep them safe.

She had no money. Derrick didn't have access to Red's accounts, but Red's lawyer did. He could help Derrick—or the police—track her.

She'd have to get as much cash as she could as fast as possible. Once they settled somewhere, she wouldn't be able to access Red's accounts.

What choice did she have, though? She'd figure something out.

Back inside, she checked on Red. His head lolled forward in

the kitchen chair. She grabbed the bottles of Gatorade she'd purchased earlier and set them in the trunk. One less thing she'd have to buy.

She rushed up the stairs and grabbed his walker. She looked around at his room. What was she forgetting? She couldn't think straight. After another moment of concentration, she shook it off. As long as she had his medications, they should be able to replace everything else.

In the kitchen, she set the walker in front of Red and shook his shoulder gently. "We need to go."

He was confused, but he didn't argue as she helped him stand and walked him to her car. He didn't even complain that they weren't taking the Cadillac.

She got her purse, took one last look around the house, and then returned to the car and sat behind the wheel. She pressed the button to open the garage door and backed into the driveway.

The dark sedan was parked in front of the neighbors' house again. That creepy feeling of being watched followed her right now, but was that a surprise?

She had been watched. She'd been followed to the grocery store.

She was being watched right now.

At the street, she turned toward the highway. Red's house, the house she'd called home for months, faded in the rearview mirror.

Had it been so wrong to wish for a home? For a family? Maybe Red wasn't her grandfather, but she loved him. Being estranged from her own parents and brothers had left her adrift. Red had given her a safe place, a solid foundation. Now, even that was gone.

Her security was gone.

Her dream of reconciling with her own family was gone.

If she wasn't careful, her freedom would be gone, too. Evaporate like mist and leave her shackled and alone.

She didn't know where they would go or what they would do. All she knew is that, one way or another, she'd keep Red safe. As long as he was safe, she could take whatever consequences came her way.

THE END.

~

Preorder Beauty in Hiding

Harper's second chance at life will become a second stint in prison if anyone connects those two dead men to her.

NUTFIELD, New Hampshire, is as good a place as any to hide from the murderer Harper left behind in Maryland. All she has to do is lie low and make enough money to keep herself and Red alive until she can figure out who her enemies are.

Jack Rossi is mystified by his beautiful new tenant and her confused grandfather. Something's not right, but the love he sees between them and the care she takes of the old man convinces Jack they're trustworthy. As drawn as he is to Harper, she's his tenant, so she's off limits.

Derrick, Harper's ex-boyfriend and Red's grandson, needs to find his grandfather and get his hands on the old man's money before Derrick ends up with a bullet in the skull. And when he gets his hands on Harper, she'll be sorry for what she's put him through.

Harper and Jack grow closer, but so do her enemies. If the truth comes out, she may lose her freedom—or her life.

Preorder *Beauty in Hiding* today.

ACKNOWLEDGMENTS

Thank you to my critique partners, Normandie Fischer, Kara Hunt, Jericha Kingston, Candice Sue Patterson, Sharon Srock, Pegg Thomas, and Terri Weldon. Great writing is ten percent talent, ten percent hard work, and 80 percent having friends like you.

Thank you to my editor, Ray Rhamey.

Thank you to my husband and children for encouraging me to follow my dreams.

Finally and most importantly, thank you, Lord, for the story and for the guidance as I struggled to make it work.

DEAR READER

If you liked BEAUTY IN FLIGHT, would you take a moment and leave me a review on Amazon, Goodreads, and your favorite retailer? Then tell all your friends. I'd be so grateful.

I started this story with the goal of writing a shorter book than I had before. But the story kept getting more and more complex until I had to break it into three books. I hope you're not cursing me for the cliffhanger ending.

Sign up for my newsletter on my website for information about future books, including the next book in this series. I promise not to sell or share your email with anybody, and I promise not to send you stuff every day. I will share my life with you a bit and, of course, tell you about my books and those of friends of mine that I think you'll enjoy.

If you're not interested in getting my emails but you would like to know about my latest releases, follow me on Amazon or BookBub. They will be alert you when I have a new book coming out.

Visit me on my Facebook page. I'd love to hear from you.

Thank you for reading! Nothing makes me happier than to share my stories.

In Christ,
Robin

Connect with me:
http://robinpatchen.com

ALSO BY ROBIN PATCHEN

Beauty in Flight

Beauty in Flight
Beauty in Hiding (Coming March, 2019)
Beauty in Battle (Coming April, 2019)

Hidden Truth

Convenient Lies
Twisted Lies
Generous Lies
Innocent Lies

Other Books

Chasing Amanda
Finding Amanda
A Package Deal

Made in the
USA
Monee, IL